FLORENCE

THE

SPROUT-LOVING

FLAUTIST

BY

PHILIP WATSON

Also by Philip Watson

CHAPTER ONE

There's one thing you need to know about Florence Foulger: when this story began she was ten years old and she...

Sorry, there are *two* things you need to know about Florence Foulger: when this story began she was ten years old and she was a very, very good flute player and she...

Sorry! There are *three* things you need to know about Florence Foulger: when this story began she was ten years old, she played the flute very, very well, and, well, you're not going to believe the third thing: she *hated* sprouts.

I know, I can't believe it either. I mean, *everybody* loves sprouts, don't they?

What? *You* don't? *Really*? Oh! Well, never mind that.

There are probably lots more things you need to know about Florence, like the fact that she had dark hair, which she refused to wear in bunches or pig-tails because they made her look like a little girl, but you'll just have to find them out as we go along, otherwise we'll never get started.

The most *important* thing to know at the beginning of this story is that Florence hated sprouts. Why she (or anyone else for that matter) should hate that tasty, nutritious, diminutive green vegetable, I have no idea. After all, sprouts are a good source of vitamin C, which can help prevent you catching a cold, *and* they're also a good source of iron. Why iron is good for you, I don't know. I'd have thought too much would make you go rusty in the rain. Anyway, Florence was not interested in the benefits of eating the small spherical parcels of goodness; she *hated* them. It could have been the taste, or the texture, or even the shape. She never said. She only ever said she hated them because they were *horrible*, and she refused to discuss the matter any further. (You may know someone just like that!)

But like all mums, Florence's mum was very keen that Florence ate healthily. (By that I don't mean that all mums were keen that *Florence* ate healthily, only that they were also keen that *their* children ate healthily.) So sprouts were high up on her list of foods for Florence to eat.

Now, the thing about sprouts is that they are a winter vegetable; and that means that they grow, and are ready to eat, in the winter. You have to feel sorry for them really. I mean, if you were a vegetable I bet you'd rather be a summer one then at least you'd be warm while you were growing, although you'd still be eaten in the end, I suppose. But a *winter* vegetable has to stand out there in the freezing cold, shivering day and night until it's big enough to be picked and eaten - not much to look forward to really. And being a winter vegetable means you are ready to be eaten at Christmas, and although lots of other vegetables are ready – like carrots, for instance, which Florence quite liked - sprouts have become something of a traditional Christmas dinner essential. *Everybody* seems to expect to have sprouts with their Christmas dinner – even Florence, although she always refused to eat them.

On the Christmas Day when our story begins, Florence's mum decided to try a slightly different approach to serving the detested vegetable to her daughter. So, in an effort to distract Florence she said, 'Why don't you all start pulling your crackers while I put the food on your plates?' Dad was puzzled by the change to the normal routine but Florence was very enthusiastic, keen to find out what present would be in her cracker and what the joke would be. And then, while Dad, Florence, and her brother Sam, were pulling their crackers, Mum served the food out. But instead of putting a pile of sprouts on Florence's plate - like she did for the rest of the family - she placed just one, solitary representative of the sprout family on her daughter's plate, hidden amongst the steaming roast potatoes, parsnips, pigs in blankets, turkey, stuffing, carrots, and goodness knows what else.

But she wasn't going to fool Florence that easily, and her daughter spotted the offending vegetable as soon as Mum put her plate down in front of her (in fact, the sprout seemed to be screaming 'Look at me! Look at me! I'm disgusting! I'm going to make you sick!').

'Why have you put *that* on my plate?' the stroppy little ten-year-old girl demanded. 'I'm not going to eat it. You know I'm not. I hate sprouts!'

'Oh, go on,' replied Mum. 'Just try it... for me. If you don't like it, you don't have to finish it. Just try one little leaf.'

'No!' growled Florence. 'I won't! There's no point, I hate sprouts!'

'How do you know?' Dad asked. 'You've never even tried one.'

'I don't need to,' replied Florence. 'I know they're horrible already.'

'They *are* pretty gross,' her brother chimed in, mischievously.

'Thank you for that, Sam.' said Dad. 'That's not very helpful, although at least you can say that, because you try them every year. To be honest, I don't like them all that much, myself.'

Mum glared at Dad. 'That's not the point, is it, Dave?' she said, and then turned back to Florence, trying to look sympathetic. 'We *have* to have sprouts at Christmas, darling: it's a tradition - like helping me put up the Christmas tree, and all these decorations.' She waved her arms around, pointing out the ornaments, tinsel, and multi-coloured lights that festooned the room, and added. 'Christmas wouldn't be the same without *those*, would it?'

'That's right,' said Dad, hastening to his wife's support to make up for admitting *he* didn't the vegetable under discussion either. 'Sprouts are another one of the things that makes Christmas special, that makes it... Christmas.'

'Like watching that black and white film every Christmas Day afternoon. "It's a *Boring* Life?"' sneered Florence.

'"It's a *Wonderful* life"' corrected Dad. 'And it's not boring, it's a classic. It's the best Christmas film ever made. Possibly the best *film* ever made.'

'No, it's not!' replied Florence. 'It's in black and white!'

'Look, Florence,' Mum interrupted, soothingly. 'Let's not worry about the film. To be honest, I don't like it that much either.' Now it was *Dad's* turn to glare at *Mum*. 'But like Daddy said, it's a tradition. It's what a lot of people watch at Christmas, just like sprouts are what people eat at Christmas.'

'Exactly!' agreed Dad. 'If it wasn't for things like sprouts, and films like "It's a Wonderful Life!" what would make Christmas so special?'

'Presents!' shouted Florence and Sam in unison, their mouths full of roast potatoes and turkey.

Dad slumped back in his chair, defeated, but Mum, leaning conspiratorially towards Florence said, in as persuasive a manner as she could, 'How about this darling? You try just a *tiny* bit of that sprout for Mummy and Daddy, and we won't have to sit down and watch that film this afternoon.' Mum heard Dad choking on his turkey and stuffing at the other end of the table, but she kept her eyes on Florence, avoiding the look in *his* eyes.

'Yes, go on!' said Sam, egging his sister on. 'You can swallow it without chewing it, and then you won't taste it. It'll only take a second, and then we won't have to sit through that film *all* afternoon.'

'That's enough of that, Sam,' said Dad, sternly. 'Florence doesn't have to try the sprout if she doesn't want to.' Now *he* was avoiding *Mum's* eyes.

Florence looked from one face to the other; her Mum and brother smiling encouragingly, her Dad trying to look sympathetic, as if he suddenly agreed with her about the evil of sprouts. She thought for a moment. Her brother was right. She could try the sprout in seconds and that film seemed to drag on all afternoon!

That was it: her mind was made up. She stabbed the sprout carefully with her fork, to make sure it didn't go flying across the table, and then she began to cut the thinnest sliver she possibly could from the side of, what to her, was a disgusting, poisonous, spheroid. As she dipped it into her gravy and slowly raised it to her mouth, Sam whispered, 'Yes!' and clenched his fist, Mum smiled encouragingly, and Dad sighed sadly. He'd already watched the film twice that month, but Christmas Day wouldn't be Christmas Day without 'It's a Wonderful Life!' He'd have to watch it when the kids had gone to bed. But there was still time; the sprout wasn't in Florence's mouth yet, perhaps she'd change her mind and put the fork down. He watched hopefully, only for his hopes to be dashed as his daughter opened her mouth, pushed the fork in carefully and then withdrew it... without the slither of sprout.

That tiny slice of the orbicular green vegetable was in her mouth!

CHAPTER TWO

Florence chewed slowly, waiting for the vile taste to explode in her mouth. Her family watched and waited; all of them expecting Florence's expression to change to one of disgust. Mum was even quite prepared for Florence to spit it out. And as they watched, Florence's expression *did* change, but not to one of disgust – she was puzzled, and then surprised, and then delighted. And before anyone could say anything, she stabbed the rest of the sprout, popped it into her mouth, and chewed enthusiastically.

'It's delicious!' she exclaimed, even before she had finished chewing. And then, dragging the bowl of sprouts from the middle of the table through the debris of the pulled-crackers, and shovelling more on to her plate, she demanded, 'Why didn't you make me try these before, Mummy?'

'I *did* try sweetheart,' replied her mum. 'Every year!'

'Well you should have tried harder, they're nicer than chocolate!' said Florence, tucking into the mountain of green balls on her plate.

'Well done, sis,' said Sam. 'No rubbish black and white film now!'

'Yes, good girl,' said Dad sadly. 'Are you sure you wouldn't like to try the film as well? You might like that now.'

'No thank you, Daddy,' replied Florence firmly, between mouthfuls of sprouts.

'No, Dave,' added Mum. 'A deal's a deal. No black and white film this afternoon.'

'All right, all right, no film,' said Dad, going back to eating his dinner. Suddenly, he was finding *his* sprouts even more difficult to swallow than usual.

Eventually, they all finished their dinners and Florence and Sam helped Mum take the plates and empty bowls into the kitchen, while Dad sat back and pretended he was too full to move. He could hear a discussion going on in the kitchen, and Florence pleading with her mummy about something or other. 'Don't tell me she's decided she doesn't like Christmas pudding, now,' he thought.

Sam came back into the dining room, and, after placing only *three* pudding bowls on the table and sitting down, he said, 'You're not going to believe this.'

'What?' asked Dad. 'Where's your sister's bowl?'

'Wait and see,' replied Sam. 'Like I said, you wouldn't believe me.'

So Dad sat and waited until Mum came in, carrying a tray with the Christmas pudding, a jug of white sauce, and a jug of yellow custard. This didn't surprise Dad, because Florence didn't like the white sauce and she always had custard on her Christmas pudding. What *did* surprise him, was Florence coming in after Mum, carrying her own bowl very carefully in two hands, as though she was afraid of spilling something. It was only when she approached the table and put the bowl down, that he could see that it was almost overflowing with sprouts!

'What! Sprouts?' he exclaimed. 'For pudding?'

'I know,' sighed Mum. 'But she insisted. I just hope she doesn't get sick of them and refuse to eat them ever again.'

'I won't!' said Florence. 'I love them.'

Mum shook her head in disbelief, but made no comment as she served out large

11

portions of Christmas pudding to the rest of her family. Florence sat politely, waiting until everyone else had been served, but as soon as Mum said, 'Help yourselves to white sauce or custard,' Florence's arm shot out, grabbed the custard, and poured it all over her sprouts!

'What are you *doing*?' gasped Mum. 'You can't eat sprouts with custard. They'll taste disgusting. You've ruined them, you silly girl!'

'No, I haven't,' said Florence. 'I love sprouts, and I love custard. So I'll love this.' And she scooped up a huge spoonful and shovelled it into her mouth. As she chewed she said, 'Mmmm' and when she swallowed she added, 'Dee-licious!' before promptly scooping up another custard–covered sprout and popping it into her mouth.

Now Mum, Dad, and Sam, *all* shook their heads and tried to eat their puddings without looking at the disgusting concoction Florence was devouring. Soon, Florence's bowl was empty, and she had to sit politely once again waiting for everyone else to finish, then she turned to her mum and said, 'Thank you for a delicious dinner, Mummy. It was the best one I've ever had.'

'Thank you, darling,' Mum replied. 'I think you've had enough sprouts to last you until next year, don't you?'

'Oh no, Mummy,' said Florence. 'I want sprouts every day now. They're scrummy, and you've always said that they are really good for me.'

'Ye...s, I did, didn't I?' said Mum, smiling nervously. 'Good job I have enough for tomorrow then, I suppose.' And, looking around the table she added, 'Well, let's not forget our other Christmas tradition: you lot clear up and put the dishwasher on, while I go and relax in the lounge.' And with that, she left her family to it.

A little while later, Mum was joined by her husband and children for a discussion about what they could do - now that they wouldn't be watching, 'It's a Wonderful Life!'. Dad suggested watching, 'Miracle on 34th Street' – the 1947, black and white version – which he said was another classic Christmas film, but nobody agreed with him. Instead, they decided that they would play whatever game Florence wanted to play, as a reward for her finally eating some sprouts.

Now, before we go any further, there's something else you need to know about sprouts

– apart from being a good source of vitamin C and iron that is. They are one of a number of foods, usually vegetables (cauliflower is another one) which have a certain effect on your digestive system. I don't know why it is, there must be something in them, but they seem to accentuate, exaggerate, or perhaps just speed up the digestive process. 'So what?' I hear you ask. And in that case there is something you need to know about the digestive process which occurs in our stomachs. Digestion is how our bodies break down the food we eat and convert it into what we need to help us grow and give us energy; and when this happens, gases are produced in our stomachs.

Now, with sprouts, these gases seem to build up very quickly and if we didn't let them out somehow, we would explode! I think, by now, you have probably guessed what I'm talking about, because it is well-known fact that everybody does it – even the Queen.

That's right, we expel these gases from our bottoms! Of course, that's not how we refer to this action, we give it all sorts of names such as...

Wait! Hang on just a moment. Here is a warning for those of a nervous disposition, or parents who do not want their children to read such things: I am about to list some of the names given to the expulsion of digestive gases through our bottoms. If you don't want to read them, then simply turn to the next chapter, by which time I will have decided which of the following words I will be using in this story.

There are very many different terms for flatulation, which is the technical term for what we are currently talking about, although nobody ever says, 'Pardon me, I have just flatulated.'

Here are just a few of the more polite and common ways of saying 'flatulated'; say them quickly if you're embarrassed: broke wind, pumped, trumped, boffed, let one go, bottom burped and, of course, farted.

From now on I shall use the term, 'trumped', because I want to. Now, we can move on.

CHAPTER THREE

Florence chose 'Twister' as the game they would all play, because she was very good at it. I expect you know how to play it – there's a big plastic mat with large coloured spots on it, and somebody spins a pointer to determine where each player, in turn, has to place their right or left foot, or right or left hand. This means that you end up in all sorts of strange positions, with your legs and arms stretched out in all directions, as you lean over, or under, the other players to reach your designated coloured spot. You have to be very flexible to be good at it, which was precisely why Florence was very good at it, and precisely why Dad wasn't.

Florence decided that her brother would be the one to spin the pointer so that she could play against Mum and Dad, because it was easy for her to beat both of them. Soon, the three players were all tangled up, and it was difficult for Sam to tell which arm or leg belonged to which player – not that he cared: he was having a great time as he watched his dad try to manoeuvre his right arm from behind Mum's left leg to just behind Florence's right hand, without falling over or lifting his other arm or either leg. With a triumphal grunt Dad finally did it, although he ended up with his face perilously close to Florence's bottom. I say 'perilously close' because, as you will remember, sprouts have a certain effect on your digestive system – you know, the production of gases that have to be released? And Florence had eaten a *lot* of sprouts and she was only ten-years-old, so her tummy wasn't very big, nor was it at all used to having to deal with sprouts.

She'd been feeling a bit of a rumbling in her tummy, but had been having far too much fun playing 'Twister' to take any notice. So it was just as much of a surprise to her, as it was to her dad, when the eruptions began. At first, there was a tiny 'phtt' sort of noise, which nobody noticed, because they were all laughing, or in Dad's case grunting, too loudly. But just as they were beginning to become aware of a strange, unidentifiable smell invading the room (for which Mum was just about to blame Dad) there was a very loud explosive sort of noise – a bit like the air being let out of the biggest balloon you've ever seen, only louder, and longer, and smellier; yes, definitely smellier! It was a mixture of rotten eggs, rotting vegetables with perhaps just a hint of chocolate! Sam promptly keeled over and rolled around on the floor, laughing hysterically whilst gasping for breath and complaining about weapons of mass destruction. The three 'Twister' players immediately collapsed into a tangled heap, arms and legs intertwined, with poor Dad's head pressed hard against Florence's bottom, which was still imitating that big balloon so vigorously that it was making Dad's cheeks wobble.

'Dave!' shouted Mum. 'That's disgusting! Can't you control yourself?'

Dad replied with a muffled choking, 'It wasn't me!'

Of course, Mum didn't believe her husband. She was well used to this sort of thing from him, although even by his standards this was nothing short of spectacular – spectacularly disgusting and noisy, that is – but with their three bodies so entangled, it was impossible to tell which one was really responsible. Mum was also certain that her sweet, little ten-year-old daughter's body was not capable of producing the foul smelling gas, which by now had just about excluded all of the breathable air from the room.

Dad extricated himself from the jumble of arms and legs on the 'Twister' mat and managed to get on to all fours before repeating his denial. 'It wasn't me! Honest!' Actually, he wasn't completely sure, because he had, in fact, been unable to prevent a small trump from his own bottom. But surely such a small emission couldn't have caused such a stench, and anyway, it had been completely silent. And you could hardly blame him for emitting such a small trump - not after a huge Christmas dinner with the usual sprouts and stuffing and... sprouts! That was it! He looked at Florence. She was now on her feet looking as sheepish as the sweetest little red-faced lamb you've ever seen. 'Sorry, Mummy,' she mumbled into her chest. 'I think it was me!'

'Don't be silly, Florence. A little girl like you couldn't...'

'Sprouts, Claire!' interrupted Dad. 'Florence ate about two tonnes of the things. They're bound to have an effect!'

'No, don't try to blame Florence,' replied Mum. 'The sprouts might have given her wind, but she couldn't possibly...'

'Thpthpthpthpthp!' Before she could finish her sentence, Mum was interrupted by another rasping crescendo from her daughter's bottom.

'Excuse me, Mummy,' whispered Florence. 'I'm sorry, I can't help it. My tummy is gurgling so much and I just can't stop trumping.' She was also finding it difficult not to giggle.

Sam could stand it no longer, he got to his feet, clamped his hand over his mouth, and made a great show of staggering out of the room. 'Air!' he cried. 'I need air!'

'Oh sweetheart,' said Mummy, giving Florence a hug. 'It's my fault, I shouldn't have let you eat so many sprouts. Does your tummy hurt?'

'A bit,' Florence replied quietly, surprised she was getting so much sympathy after creating such a smell, but quickly deciding to make the most of it. 'Can I sit down and watch the tele?'

'Yes, I think you should,' said Mummy. 'Perhaps 'Twister' wasn't the best game to play after eating so many sprouts.'

Quickly seizing the opportunity, Dad offered, 'Shall I put "It's a Wonderful Life" on then?'

'No!' said Mum and Florence simultaneously.

'Oh,' said a disappointed Dad. 'What then? I could see if "Gone With the *Wind*" is on?'

'Not funny, Dave' replied Mum. 'Come on, let's go and choose a DVD, Florence. Dave, you can put the game away.'

As Florence and Mum left the room, and Dad knelt down to start folding up the 'Twister' mat, he couldn't resist calling after his wife and daughter, 'What about "*Wind* in the Willows" then?'

'Still not funny, Dave' came the reply. 'And you can make a cup of tea when you've finished in there.'

Dad did as he was told, and the three of them were soon drinking cups of tea watching the film Florence had chosen. Florence was cuddled up to Mum on the sofa, whilst Dad sat as far away as he discretely could, as Florence's bottom was still 'popping' at regular intervals, with the accompanying putrid odour. Sam made one entrance into the room but immediately pretended to choke on the smell and retreated back to his bedroom, only coming down briefly at teatime to pick up some food and take it straight back upstairs.

Florence's trumping continued for the rest of afternoon and evening, which made her bath-time great fun as she was blowing bubbles constantly from her bottom. Things in her tummy finally seemed to be settling down by the time she went to bed, and as she was being tucked in, Florence asked, 'Will my tummy do that every time I have sprouts, Mummy?'

'I don't think so darling,' replied Mummy. 'You did eat rather a lot today, and you weren't used to them. If you still want some tomorrow, you can just have a few and we'll see what happens.'

'Thank you, Mummy, night-night,' said Florence as Mum kissed her.

'Night-night, sweetheart,' said Mum. 'Sleep tight.'

And that's exactly what Florence did, dreaming about huge, delicious mountains of sprouts, as her duvet gently wafted in the breezes from her popping bottom.

CHAPTER FOUR

The following morning, being the day after Christmas Day, was Boxing Day, so called because of the number of boxing matches that break out in families on that day – either that, or because rich people used to give boxes as presents to their servants; although what the servants did with these boxes I have no idea. Anyway, on *this* Boxing Day, Florence woke up quite early in her very smelly bedroom. Luckily for her she couldn't smell it, as she'd been breathing in the rather noxious fumes all night and her nose had become desensitised. The same thing couldn't be said of her mum, who got a whiff of it as she walked past the door and burst in thinking that some poor animal must have crawled in weeks ago and passed away under the bed, unnoticed. Of course, as soon as she stepped into the room she recognised the smell, shot across to the window and opened it wide.

'Mummy!' cried Florence, pulling her 'Princess' duvet over herself. 'What have you done that for? It's freezing!'

'The smell, of course,' replied Mum. 'Can't you smell it? It's awful.'

'No,' said Florence. 'I can't smell a thing.'

Mum frowned momentarily, taking care to stay by the open window, before saying, 'Oh, your nose must've got used to it. How *is* your tummy, by the way, still gurgling?'

Florence put her hand on her stomach before replying, 'No, Mummy. I think it's stopped.'

'That's a relief,' said Mum. 'Daddy and I were beginning to worry last night, when you just kept trumping and trumping.'

'Can I have some sprouts today, then?' asked Florence, hopefully.

'Perhaps a few,' replied Mum.

'For breakfast?' Florence suggested. 'With milk on?'

'No!' Mum replied firmly. 'You can have some at lunchtime – with gravy on, like everyone else... if your tummy behaves until then. If it doesn't, then you won't have any then either. Grandma and Grandad are coming for lunch, and we can't have you making that sort of smell in front of them – not at their age! Now come on, let's go and get some breakfast... and leave your window open.'

So Mum and Florence had their breakfast – boring cereals with milk, not delicious sprouts – and then, when she was dressed, Florence sat in the living room watching a DVD she'd been given for Christmas. She was eventually joined by Dad, who greeted her with a kiss on the head and a, 'Good morning, trumpy bottom. Mummy tells me you're better now. That's a relief!'

'Yes, I am, and Mummy says I can have some sprouts at lunchtime,' replied Florence.

'But not for pudding as well?' said Dad, a touch of horror mixed in with the question in his voice.

'I hope so,' said Florence. 'They're delicious with custard on.'

Dad shuddered at the thought just as Mum entered the room and said, 'No, not for pudding, not with custard or white sauce, or even with jelly. I've told you already, you can have a *few* sprouts with gravy on and that's it. We don't want your tummy getting upset again like yesterday.'

'But it's better now!' Florence protested.

'And I want to keep it that way,' said Mum. 'Grandma and Grandad have just rung; they're on their way over, should be about half-an-hour. Has that DVD nearly finished? You know how they always have something to say about how much television you watch.'

'It's not television. It's a DVD. It's not the same,' said Florence.

'It is to them,' replied Mum. 'So why don't you get your flute out? They love it when you play for them.'

'I'll go and get it when this has finished, there's not long left' said Florence happily – she loved playing for Grandma and Grandad; they always listened with great beaming smiles on their faces.

Mum went back to the kitchen to count out the sprouts she was going to be cooking; she didn't want to do too many and give Florence the chance of asking for more. So she wasn't in the room when Florence began to squirm about on the sofa, and Dad was too engrossed in the DVD to notice Florence's wriggling, or the worried look on her face. Florence's tummy had started to gurgle again and worse than that, it felt like her bottom was about to start popping again. She was torn between rushing off to her bedroom to trump in secret, and staying to watch the end of the DVD. The film had reached a really exciting bit, but if she stayed she risked Dad noticing her squirming, as she clenched her bottom cheeks together as tightly as she could, or, worse still, she might start trumping, filling the room with that awful stench: then Mum would find out and not let her have any sprouts.

As the pressure in her bottom increased Florence realised she couldn't take the risk and she leapt to her feet, 'Need a wee!' she fibbed, as she sprinted from the room.

'Why do you always leave it until the last minute?' replied Dad. 'I'll put it on pause for you.'

'Thank you!' Florence yelled, from half way up the stairs. On the landing she looked towards the bathroom; the door was closed – Sam was finally out of bed, so she threw open her bedroom door, slamming it shut behind her. She leant against the door as she relaxed the now rather tired muscles, which had been clenching her bottom cheeks together so tightly. But her relief was short-lived, as she realised there was trouble brewing in her tummy: the beginnings of a tremendous rasping explosion emitting from her bottom. This one would be heard all over the house – if not all over the town. The pressure must have been building up as she squashed her bottom cheeks together watching the DVD. What could she do? She immediately tried squeezing her cheeks together again, but all that did was change the noise to a high pitched whistle. She had to muffle the noise! So she grabbed her duvet, scrunched it up as much as she could and sat on it, relaxing her 'bottom muscles' with a great sigh of relief. The duvet worked; there was barely a sound as she trumped longer and louder than she had done all day yesterday. At least, she presumed it would have been louder from the way her bottom vibrated - even cushioned by her duvet – and, as she sat and waited for the volcanic rumblings to subside she realised that in much the same way as the pressure had built up in her tummy, the smell must be now building up in the folds of her duvet. She would have to deal with that quickly, before it seeped out under her bedroom door and rolled down the stairs to Mum's over-sensitive nostrils.

As soon as she could no longer feel the tiniest eruption from her bottom, Florence took a huge breath, grabbed her duvet, and pushed and shoved it through her open window, taking care to hold on to one end of it. It was a very windy day and Florence's duvet waved around like a sail in a hurricane, flapping around in front of her face - so she didn't see her grandma and grandad pull up on to the drive below her window. They gawped through the windscreen, wondering why on earth their normally very sensible granddaughter was waving at them with her duvet. At the same time, Florence heard Mum calling, 'Florence! Sam! Grandma and Grandad are here. Come on down!'

Caught by surprise, Florence turned in panic in case Mum came into her bedroom looking for her, and her grip loosened on her duvet. Before she knew what was happening, it had slipped from her grasp and she watched in horror as the wind took it, tossed it around for a few seconds before getting bored and dropping it on to Grandad's windscreen. For a moment, Florence stared aghast at her duvet, which seemed to be caught on the windscreen wipers. Then she pulled herself together, turned and sprinted out of her bedroom and down the stairs in the hope she could grab her duvet before her mum saw it.

But Mum was already at the bottom of the stairs waiting for her.

CHAPTER FIVE

'Oh no!' thought Florence. 'She'll see my duvet, and then she'll ask how it got on to Grandad's windscreen and...' Her thoughts were cut short by Mum saying, 'We'll not mention what happened yesterday, Florence: after you ate all those sprouts.'

'OK,' replied a breathless Florence. 'I'm sure it won't happen again, anyway. You know, the strangest thing just happened...'

'Did it, darling?' said Mum. 'Tell me about it in a minute. I don't want to leave Grandma and Grandad standing outside, freezing on the doorstep.' And with that she opened the front door for her parents, who were both carrying large bags full of Christmas presents. Grandad also had Florence's duvet tucked under his arm.

'Hello, Merry Christmas!' said Grandma.

'Merry Christmas to you too,' replied Mum. 'What's that you've got under your arm, Dad? It looks like Florence's duvet!'

'It is!' said Florence as she leapt forward, hugged her grandad whilst wishing him a 'Merry Christmas', and pulled the duvet from his grasp. 'It fell out of my window when I was... when I was trying to...'

Fortunately, before Florence could complete her sentence (which was going to be something pathetic about wanting to see if her duvet would make a good flag) Sam appeared at the top of the stairs and called, 'Merry Christmas Grandma and Grandad! Wait 'til you hear about "Farty Florence" and her amazing burping bottom!'

Grandad spluttered out a laugh, but before he had chance to express his interest in Sam's proposed topic of conversation, Mum interrupted with, 'That's enough of that, Sam. I'm sure Grandma and Grandad don't want to hear anything of the sort. Now come on down and make them a nice cup of tea.' She gave her mum a hug and added, 'Unless you'd like a pre-dinner sherry, Mum?'

Grandma looked at Grandad, and then at Sam, who was ambling downstairs with a mischievous grin on his face, as Florence was sprinting (and tripping over her duvet) on her way upstairs, and decided that it could be one of 'those' afternoons, so she replied, 'A sherry would be very nice, Claire, thank you.'

When he reached the bottom of the stairs Sam hugged his grandad first, and complimented him on his Christmas jumper - with its reindeer with a flashing red nose. Then he turned and hugged his grandma, and, knowing that she'd been to the hairdressers on Christmas Eve, said, 'Your hair looks nice, Grandma.'

Grandma responded as she always did, with a huge smile, but said, 'Thank you, Sam; I wish I could say the same thing about yours. It looks like you've just got out of bed.'

Sam pretended to look offended, but his mum explained. 'I know! But it's *supposed* to look like that! He's spent half an hour in the bathroom using the hair gel we gave him yesterday to make it look like he's just got out of bed!'

Grandma shook her head and said, 'I don't know... kids today! What's wrong with a bit of water and a brush and comb?'

By now, an even more breathless Florence had returned and Dad had come out of the living room to say 'Hello,' having first switched off the television, so it was suddenly very crowded in the hallway.

'Why are we all standing out here?' said Mum. 'Sam, go and put the kettle on, while the rest of us go into the living room. Oh, and bring the mince pies back with you. I'm sure Grandma and Grandad would like one.'

'Should I bring a sprout pie for Florence?' replied Sam, as he turned to do his mum's bidding.

Florence blushed, Dad failed to supress a smile, and Mum shook her head as she sighed, 'Just put the kettle on, and stop being silly.'

'Sprout pie?' said an intrigued Grandad. 'Who's been baking sprout pies? Not Florence, that's for sure.'

'Nobody, it's just Sam being Sam,' said Mum, as she ushered everyone through the door into the living room. 'Now Mum, you sit there and Dad, you sit there. Florence, you fetch their presents from under the tree. Dave, you get Mum a nice glass of sherry.'

'Well, I'm not going to get her a horrible one, am I?' said Dad. 'Especially as she's my *favourite* mother-in-law.'

'Don't *you* start,' said Mum. 'Sam's bad enough.'

Dad ignored the comment and replied, 'Would *you* like a sherry as well, light of life, oasis of my desert? I think *I'll* have a small beer, if I may.'

'Make sure it is a small one and, yes, I will have a sherry,' said Mum.

Dad poured two large sherries, knowing that his wife and mother-in-law would both protest (which they did) but that both would drink them without a problem (which they also did). Then he disappeared into the kitchen to fetch his beer just as Sam entered carrying a plate of mince pies and announced that the kettle was on.

Soon, the whole family was sitting, more or less in a circle, swapping presents, which consisted of the usual assortment of clothes, vouchers, and chocolates: Mum and Grandma sipping sherry, Grandad sipping tea, Dad drinking beer, and Sam and Florence drinking orange squash. Dad topped up Mum's and Grandma's sherries, while the presents' opening continued with a 'Wow!' or a 'Just what I wanted' or a 'Well, I never know what to get you' (as another voucher was revealed) or a 'You shouldn't have,' which in Dad's case he meant – he really didn't like that particular aftershave; the one his mother-in-law bought him every year. Still, the staff in the local charity shop would be very grateful for it. They always were: he was pretty sure they used to it to clean the metal bits-and-bobs that people brought in as donations.

Mum's diversion tactics had worked: Grandad forgot all about Sam's curious references to Florence and sprout pie while they opened their presents. In fact, it was not until he was sitting next to Florence at the dining table and he saw that she had several sprouts on her plate that Grandad remembered. 'Sprouts, Florence? You don't *like* sprouts. Are you being punished for something?'

'No,' replied his granddaughter, proudly. 'I *love* sprouts. They're delicious.'

'Since when?' asked Grandad.

'Since yesterday,' Sam chimed in, ignoring the look he got from Mum. 'She can't get enough of them. Even had them for pudding.'

'Good grief!' said Grandad. Then he turned to Florence and added in wise sort of voice, but with a sparkle in his eye, 'You should be careful eating too many sprouts Florence. They can make you...' He leaned over and whispered in her ear, 'Trump!'

'A toast!' Mum exclaimed, a little more loudly than she'd intended, raising the glass of sparkling wine, which had now replaced her empty sherry glass. 'Merry Christmas, everybody!'

'Merry Christmas!' everyone replied, raising their own glasses.

Then, picking his cracker up, Grandad turned to Florence and said, 'Shall we, Princess?' So she did, and so did everyone else. And before long they were all wearing their paper hats and reading the silly jokes they found in their crackers, which, for some reason, Grandma and Mum seemed to find funnier than everyone else. Not that Florence noticed: she was too busy tucking into her delicious sprouts, so that in no time they were gone, and she was picking at the rest of her dinner in a most unenthusiastic manner.

'You really do like sprouts, don't you, Florence?' said Grandad.

'Yes,' she replied. 'They're absolutely scrummy!'

'Well, I'll let you into a little secret,' Grandad whispered, leaning over in a conspiratorial sort of way. 'I can't stand them. Just hang on a minute; keep eating.' Then he caught Sam's eye and winked at him, before turning to his wife and saying, 'Betty, I think you offended your grandson when you said his hair looked like he'd just got out of bed. Isn't that right, Sam?'

Sam hadn't a clue what his grandad was up to but he knew it would be fun, so he agreed, 'Mortally wounded, I was, Grandma.'

Grandma looked at Sam in horror. 'What? Oh no, Sam,' she said. 'I didn't mean it. I was only joking. Your hair looks... very... fashionable!'

Sam looked hurt again. 'Fashionable?' he whined. 'I don't want to look fashionable. I want to look... cool... like I don't care about being fashionable!'

'That's what I meant,' said Grandma hastily. '*Un*fashionable! That's how it looks.'

'Unfashionable?' Sam moaned. 'That's even worse.'

Seeing her mother's confusion, Mum addressed her son. 'Sam, what are you talking about? That sort of hair is *very* fashionable. I thought that was why you wanted the gel.'

'It's not gel. It's *wax!*' Sam protested.

Dad was also confused, but was quite happy to sit back, sipping his beer and watch the obvious discomfort of his mother-in-law.

So none of them saw Grandad tipping his plate slightly and silently scraping his sprouts off on to Florence's plate; nor did they notice Florence woofing them down. And it was not until she'd finished her illicit extra portion of sprouts that Grandad interrupted the conversation with, 'Well, I'm sure Grandma didn't mean any offense, Sam.'

'That's all right, none taken,' replied Sam, raising his glass of juice to his grandad and winking, before tucking in once more to his own dinner.

Mum looked at Grandma, who stared back, nonplussed. Then she looked at Dad who shrugged, smiled, and said, 'More wine?' Mum nodded; Grandma simply held her glass out.

The rest of meal was eaten mainly in silence, apart from Grandad and Florence, who chatted happily about Florence's flute playing. When it was time for the pudding, Sam asked if he could have sprouts and custard, and Grandma was very surprised when her daughter giggled, as she answered, 'No, you may not.'

Florence knew that she'd had more than her sprout ration for the day, so she made no fuss about only being offered Christmas pudding, and ate it all up without a murmur. Unfortunately, she could feel ominous rumblings beginning in her tummy again, so she was mortified when, as soon as everyone had finished eating Sam, not-so-innocently piped up, 'Mum, can we play Twister again, this afternoon?'

CHAPTER SIX

Of course, there was never *any* chance of Mum agreeing to a game of 'Twister', despite her husband offering to drop out so that his mother-in-law could play. Although she did giggle at the thought of her mother experiencing Florence's sprout-induced eruptions in the middle of the game, just as her husband had done the day before - with her face right next to Florence's bottom. However, Sam's alternative suggestion of 'Charades' was perfectly acceptable to everyone, especially when he offered to make up some titles for everyone else to act out.

Meanwhile, Florence's tummy was continuing to rumble and she knew it was only a matter of time before she could control it no longer. 'Mummy,' she said. 'Can I go up and practice my flute, instead of playing "Charades"? I told Grandad I'd play some carols for him this afternoon, and I want to make sure I know them.'

'Of course you know them!' Mum replied. 'You had to learn them for your school concert, and they are *so* simple.'

'But I want to make sure they're perfect for Grandma and Grandad' Florence pleaded.

While Mum and Florence were talking, Dad caught a whiff of something decidedly unpleasant, which in previous years he'd have been sure had emanated from Grandad, but after the events of the previous afternoon he wasn't so sure. It definitely had Florence's signature scent attached, and he had no desire to experience the full aroma again. 'Oh, let her go, Claire,' he chimed in. 'You and I can play against your mum and dad. It'll keep the sides even.'

Florence didn't wait for Mum to agree; she shot off, leaving Grandad gaping in amazement. 'Blimey, she's keen.' he said. 'She really doesn't have to practice so hard for us.' He'd hardly finished his sentence when he heard Florence's bedroom door slam: she was in too much of a rush to worry about closing her door quietly and flew across the room, plonked herself down on her duvet, which she'd left in a heap on her bed, and relaxed. The duvet did its job once again and muffled the noise and vibrations – at least sufficiently for them not to be heard downstairs. A smile of relief crossed her face as she felt the pressure in her tummy reduce. 'Ahh!' she sighed. 'That's better.' And then, after a few minutes, when she was sure the explosions had ceased, she once again shoved the duvet out of her window to get rid of the smell, making sure this time that she didn't let go of it. Eventually, Florence dragged the duvet back inside, picked up her flute and practiced the carols she was going to play for her grandparents.

Downstairs, Grandad heard Florence begin to play, looked up at the ceiling and said proudly, 'Beautiful. You were right Claire, she didn't have to practice.' Claire didn't reply: she was giggling as she watched her husband mime 'crying' and 'being a tree' at the same time. Knowing how Sam's mind worked, she'd already worked out that her husband trying to do 'Wind in the Willows'. Dave was obviously trying to be a 'weeping willow'. This was the fourth title they'd acted out between them and every one had had the word 'wind' in it. Whether it was Dave's rubbish miming, or her mother's obvious bemusement at the repetition of the word 'wind', that Claire found so funny, she couldn't say, but she couldn't stop laughing. Finally, she put her husband out of his misery and shouted, 'Wind in the Willows!'

Grandma looked at Grandad and said, 'Have you noticed how everything has "wind" in the title, George?'

'Yes, dear,' Grandad replied. 'I think it's Sam's theme for the game; perhaps to make it easier for us.'

Mum laughed even louder at this, and Dad realised it was time to call a halt to the game. 'Sam, go and tell your sister, Grandma and Grandad can't wait any longer for her to play for them.'

'But there's one you haven't done yet,' Sam complained. 'It's a good one.

'I'm sure it is,' replied Dad. 'And I bet it's got "wind" in the title.'

'How did you know?' gasped Sam.

'Never mind that, go and get your sister,' said Dad.

Sam dutifully bounded upstairs, threw Florence's door open without knocking, sniffed the air, looked at the open window, and said, 'I hope you're better now. They're ready for your recital.' Then he bounced back downstairs only to be told to go and put the kettle and make some coffee for Mum and Grandma. Having done that, he brought the two cups into the living room to find everyone, including Florence, waiting for him.

'Here he is,' said Grandma. 'Knew you wouldn't want to miss your sister playing, so we waited for you.'

'Gosh, thanks,' replied Sam, putting the coffees down, dropping into a chair and picking up his mobile phone.

Florence looked round her small, attentive audience, glared at Sam, and then put her flute to her lips and began to play. First of all, she played 'Silent Night', which was really easy but was her Grandma's favourite carol. When she'd finished everyone clapped, except for Sam, who seemed to be oblivious to it all. Florence smiled proudly and then said, 'Now I'll play, "Ding Dong Merrily On High" – for Grandad, because it's *his* favourite.' And off she went, her fingers dancing across the keys of her flute. Grandma and Grandad were smiling broadly, and singing along. Mum was beaming, grateful that everything was going so well and that Florence's tummy seemed to be behaving itself today. Dad sat back, proud of his daughter and happily sipping his beer. Sam, head down, was happily playing some game or other on his mobile phone. The only person who wasn't entirely happy was Florence. Her tummy was starting to rumble again, and she was having difficulty concentrating on her flute playing whilst having to squeeze her bottom cheeks together. Soon she was squirming and rocking from side to side, even standing on one leg for a time.

'Why is standing on one leg?' asked Grandma, leaning over to her husband. 'She reminds of that flute player from years ago, used to stand on one leg.'

'Hopalong Cassidy?' said Grandad, impishly.

'No!' said Grandma, elbowing her husband in the ribs. 'You *know* who I mean, you're just being... Jethro Tull! That's who I mean.' *(See note at the end of the chapter)*

Florence had reached the last chorus – the 'Glo-o-o-o-o-o-ri-a' bit - when, despite nipping her cheeks together as tightly as she could, she could hold it in no longer and a 'squeak' escaped. And then another. And then another, at a slightly higher pitch as she squeezed her bottom even more tightly. Then another popped out at a lower pitch, as her tired bottom muscles relaxed slightly. But the amazing thing was, nobody seemed to notice. In fact, Grandma and Grandad seemed even more impressed than ever, and clapped incredibly loudly when she'd finished.

'Wow!' said Grandad. 'How did you do that? It was brilliant!'

'Yes, it was darling,' agreed Mum. 'I've never heard you play like that before.'

Even Sam looked up from his phone, impressed.

'Do what?' asked Florence.

'Make it sound like you were playing a trumpet as well as a flute,' explained Mum. 'How do you get the flute to sound like that?

'It was like you were playing a duet with yourself,' said Grandma. 'It was *really* clever.'

'They're right, Florence,' joined in Dad. 'That's the best you've ever played.

But as Florence's audience all stared at her in appreciation, a distinctive fragrance began to pervade the room.

NOTE AT THE END OF THE CHAPTER

Jethro Tull was a very clever farmer who was born in 1674 and invented lots of things to make farming more efficient, but he's not who Grandma meant. She meant the legendary classic rock band of the 1960s and 70s, whose lead singer often stood on one leg while playing his flute; obviously, he wasn't singing at the time (or inventing farm machinery).

CHAPTER SEVEN

Grandma looked at Grandad and frowned at him in disgust. 'George!' she hissed.

'Don't look at me,' George replied, feigning deep hurt, whilst finding it very funny. He looked at his son-in-law, who held his hands up and said, 'Not me either, George.'

Sam, meanwhile, had curled up in fits of laughter in his armchair. 'Oh, Sam!' said Grandma, sounding disappointed. But Sam just managed to gasp, 'Not me, Grandma.'

Mum, of course, knew exactly who was responsible. She looked at her daughter with a mixture of horror, deepest sympathy, and if she were honest, childish amusement. Florence stood stock-still, arms by her side, flute dangling in her right hand, her face the deepest shade of crimson and her eyes full of tears. She was momentarily paralysed with dismay: she'd disgusted her Grandma, embarrassed her mum in front of her parents, and showed that she could not stop herself trumping if she ate sprouts. She'd never be allowed to eat them again. She ran from the room, sobbing.

Grandma and Grandad looked at their daughter for an explanation. 'It's the sprouts,' she responded. 'She ate loads yesterday, including – like Sam said – for pudding! Then she couldn't stop trumping. Started in the middle of a game of "Twister".'

'Don't remind me,' Dad interrupted. 'I've still got the smell in my nostrils.' He took out a tissue and blew his nose, as if trying to rid himself of a lingering odour.

Mum gave him what he called a 'dirty look', before continuing. 'And as Dave was so graphically describing, the smell was horrendous. It seemed to have settled down this morning, so I said she could have some sprouts today, but I was careful to only let her have a few. She must be very sensitive to them.'

'Ah,' said Grandad. 'She may *not* be over-sensitive. She may have had a few more sprouts than you thought, Claire.'

Mum gave him a puzzled look. Grandma raised a single, accusing, eyebrow.

'You see,' Grandad went on. 'When I found out how much she likes them... and I *don't*, not really... I smuggled mine on to her plate while you were all talking about Sam's hair!'

'But I thought you liked sprouts!' exclaimed Mum. 'That's why I always give you so many.'

'I know,' replied Grandad. 'But I've never had the heart to tell you.'

'So she's had a double portion... again!' said Mum. 'More than that – because I gave *you* so many.'

'I'm afraid so,' sighed Grandad. 'Sorry. I'll go and see how she is and apologise.'

With that, Grandad used the arm of the sofa to push himself to his feet and went to see his granddaughter. The living room fell silent as Mum, Dad and Grandma all thought about how upset Florence had been. Even Sam was quiet for a few moments until he piped up, 'But did you hear the sounds she made when she trumped? They were exactly in tune with what she was playing. It was amazing.'

'That's enough of that, Sam,' replied his mum. 'Think about your little sister, for once.'

'I am!' retorted Sam. 'My mates would pay a fortune to hear her perform like that. They'd be so jealous of her.'

'Don't even *think* about telling anyone,' ordered Mum. 'And don't you *dare* put anything on social media.'

'I *won't*,' said Sam. 'I was only saying.'

'Well don't,' said Mum. And silence fell on the room once more.

Upstairs, Grandad knocked on Florence's door and was greeted by a, 'Go away!'

'It's me... Grandad,' he replied. 'I've come to say, "Sorry".'

'What for?' asked Florence.

'Can I come in and explain?' asked Grandad.

'All right,' said Florence. 'I suppose so.'

He opened the door to be hit by the most obnoxious smell he'd ever encountered. He felt like he'd have to hack his way through it to get into the room. And while he did his best not to overreact, he couldn't disguise the expression of pain and nausea on his face, although he refused to allow himself to cover his nose with his handkerchief. This wasn't Florence's fault. She saw the look on his face and said despondently, 'I know! But I've left the window open!'

'Never mind,' said Grandad, as he sat down on the bed next to her. 'You can't help it. It's my fault. I shouldn't have given you all those extra sprouts.'

'I shouldn't have eaten them,' replied Florence, 'after what happened yesterday.'

Grandad said nothing, and they sat in silence for a little while before Florence said, 'I trumped right in Daddy's face, while we were playing "Twister". His face was squashed right up against my bottom!'

Grandad couldn't stop himself laughing, and soon Florence joined in. 'It *was* funny,' she said. 'Although Mummy and Daddy didn't think so.'

'So that's what all that squirming and standing on one leg was about? You... trying to hold your trumps in,' said Grandad.

'Yes,' agreed Florence. 'But I couldn't, and then ...'

'And then when they did sneak out it sounded like you were playing two instruments. It really was amazing. So many of your trumps were exactly in tune. And you weren't even trying... were you?'

'No,' said Florence. 'I was just squeezing my bottom to try to keep them in.'

'You know what you are, don't you?' said Grandad.

'What?' asked Florence.

'You're a flatulist, that's what.' said Grandad.

''A what?' said Florence.

'A flatulist,' Grandad repeated. 'That's someone who can play tunes by trumping.'

'No way,' said Florence. 'That's not a real thing.'

'Yes it is,' Grandad assured her. 'Get Sam to "Google" it, if you don't believe me. Come on, let's go back down.'

'What if I start trumping again?' said Florence. 'I'm bound to.'

'No need to worry about that: the cat's out of the bag now – at least the trumps are,' laughed Grandad. 'Anyway, it's me that's in the doghouse for your trumping today, not you. Come on.'

So, leaving the bedroom window wide open, they went downstairs together. Florence received lots of sympathetic hugs from Grandma, while Grandad received dirty looks. He got another one when he asked Sam to 'Google' 'Flatulist', which his grandson was more than happy to do.

Then Sam read aloud, with great relish, from his phone, '"A flatulist, or professional farter, is an entertainer whose routine consists of passing gas in a creative, musical, or amusing manner."' He looked up at his sister. 'That's you Florence,' he added. 'Florence, the Flatulist!'

'Sam, Florence is *not* a professional farter,' said Mum.

'She could be,' Sam insisted. 'She's obviously a natural. I mean she'll need to practice; she's not perfect yet: I'm sure she hit a few *bum* notes!'

'Sam!' shouted Mum.

Taking no notice of her, Sam said, 'It says here, there's one called "Mr Methane". I bet his routine is an absolute gas!'

'Go and put the kettle, Sam,' said Mum, ignoring his second attempt at a joke. 'I'm sure Grandma and Grandad would like a cup of tea. I know I would.'

'Me too,' added Dad. 'And get yourself another juice if you like.'

'Gee, thanks Dad,' said Sam as he stood up. 'What about you Florence? I could do you a smoothie if you like, with spr- '

'Sam, just make the tea,' said Mum. She waited until Sam was out of the room before turning to Florence and saying, 'Well, sweetheart, it looks like that's all the sprouts you'll be having for a while. We can't have you trumping like that every day; especially when you're back at school. Imagine what would happen.'

'They'd have to close the school!' Sam shouted from the kitchen.

'*You're* not supposed to be listening,' Dad shouted back.

'But, Mum...' Florence protested.

'No buts,' replied Mum. 'If you can't control your tummy, you can't have sprouts.'

'They don't go back to school for a week or so, do they?' asked Grandad.

'A week tomorrow,' confirmed Mum.

'Well, why don't you let Florence have a few sprouts each day, if she wants them, and see if she can learn to control her tummy? She nearly controlled it today, even though she'd had a lot more than she should have.'

'She didn't really,' said Mum.

'She did try, though,' said Grandma, joining in on Florence's side. 'Give her a chance, Claire. It'd be a shame if she couldn't eat sprouts, especially after *you've* tried so hard every year to get her to eat them.'

'Yes,' agreed Grandad. 'Give her until next Sunday, then she'll have two days for her tummy to stop grumbling before she goes back to school - if she can't learn how to control it.'

'Ha! Well, you never have,' replied Mum. 'What do you think, Dave?'

'W..e..ll, what harm can it do?' Dad said.

'We could all be gassed to death!' Sam shouted from the kitchen.

Mum ignored her son and said to Florence, 'All right, you can have a few every day until Sunday, if you don't get sick of them. But it stops then, if you're still trumping like a…. your grandad!'

'I resent that!' cried Grandad. 'My trumps are nowhere near as smelly, or as tuneful, as Florence's.'

'Yes, all right, George,' said Grandma. 'I think we've talked about it for long enough now. Florence, did you say you'd got a DVD for Christmas? Shall we watch it?'

If Grandma was suggesting watching the television, then they all knew she'd had enough of the current topic of conversation and also knew better than to argue. So Dad put the DVD in the machine, switched the television on, and they all settled down to watch, with the cups of tea Sam brought in. Florence had to ask for it to be 'put on pause' twice, while she excused herself, but then so did Grandad.

When the film had finished Grandma and Grandad went home and Grandad gave Florence an extra tight hug and wished her luck with her tummy control. That evening, Florence was relieved to get into bed so that she could relax her bottom muscles, which were beginning to ache and, of course, she slept with her window open!

CHAPTER EIGHT

The following morning, Florence found it difficult to make herself come out from under her duvet: it was absolutely freezing in her bedroom. But eventually, she forced herself to get up and get dressed before her mum came in. Although she couldn't smell anything herself, she was certain that her mum would, and that might make her change her mind about letting Florence eat sprouts.

Unfortunately, while Florence and Dad were finishing their breakfasts (Sam was still in the bathroom making his hair look like he'd just got out of bed) Mum nipped upstairs for something. When she reappeared she said, 'I'm not sure about you having sprouts today Florence, your tummy's obviously no better. There was a *terrible* smell coming from your bedroom, so I went in to open the window and found that it already was! Goodness knows what it would have been like if it had been closed.'

'But that's because I was asleep and wasn't trying to stop it,' said Florence. 'I've not trumped since I came downstairs, have I?'

'She's right,' said Dad. 'Let's stick to the plan, Claire. I'll try to think of something to stop her bedroom smelling so much.'

Mum looked at her daughter's big, blue, pleading eyes and, not for the first time, gave in. 'All right,' she said. 'But I want to keep a close eye on you Florence. I don't want you sneaking off every five minutes because you need to trump.'

And that's what happened for the next few days: Florence spent most of her time downstairs watching television, playing with something she'd got for Christmas, or practicing on her flute; all where Mum could see, hear, and even worse... smell her!! And for the first two days, Florence did have some problems preventing her trumps escaping. She was very disappointed when this happened – as was anybody else who happened to be in the room with her – but on the third day she didn't trump at all during the day, nor on the fourth.

She'd done it. She had learnt how to stop trumping, even after she'd eaten sprouts.

Of course, the wind had to come out at some time, and not releasing it during the day meant only one thing: it had to come out at night. Fortunately, as he'd promised, Dad did do something about stopping the bedroom smelling so much: he put a fan just inside the door and set it so that it blew towards the open window. This did mean that the birds stopped perching in the tree that stood just outside the window, but at least the bedroom smelled a bit fresher.

Each evening, Florence would wait until Mum and Dad had been in to say goodnight and the door was firmly closed and then she would relax and, as her brother Sam would put it, let rip. At least she did on the first night, but she made such a racket that the pictures on her bedroom wall shook, so the next night she tried to control the noise. She relaxed her bottom, and then as soon as the noise started she clenched it again, and stopped the noise completely, repeating this until the pressure had subsided, and she felt she could go to sleep without fear of her trumps being so noisy that they would wake her, and everybody else, up!

The following night, instead of stopping the trumps completely, she decided to try to slow them down and found, that by clenching her muscles to different degrees, she could make a very high pitched sound like the highest note on her flute, or a very low one as deep as the lowest note she'd ever heard played on a tuba. And that night she went to sleep wondering if she really could become a 'flatulist' like 'Mr Methane'.

When she woke up the next morning, all Florence wanted to do was practice her new skill in the privacy of her bedroom. But Mum still wasn't totally convinced that she could control her trumping, and insisted that Florence stayed downstairs with her. So, instead, she had to spend the whole day not trumping at all. However, as soon as they'd had their tea-time meal, Florence managed to convince Mum to let her go to her room to practice on her flute – she was helped by the fact that Dad wanted to watch a football match on the television, without a flute accompaniment.

Once in her room, Florence resisted the temptation to relax her trumping muscles completely, picked up her flute and some sheet music, and began to play. She began by playing the flute on its own and then trying to let her bottom 'join in' occasionally, on the odd note. It was extremely difficult: she had to concentrate so hard on controlling her trumps that she started making mistakes on her flute, *and* she couldn't get the timing right. She found that there was a slight delay between her relaxing her muscles and the trump coming out, so that her bottom always played the note too late. In the end, she decided to put the flute down and just 'play her bottom', hoping that no one would hear. She would have to try to control the volume, as well as the pitch, of her trumps. Florence moved her music stand and sheet music over to the open window, and started to play the notes only through her bottom.

It worked!

True, she was 'playing' the music more slowly than it should have been played, and she did hit, or rather 'blow' the occasional wrong note, but she could definitely play music through her bottom! It was amazing! Wait until she showed her grandad; although she would have to do that in secret – she wasn't sure what Mum and Grandma would think. She practiced for another ten minutes, but then had to stop, because, quite frankly, she'd run out of wind, but she went to sleep a very happy ten-year-old girl.

The next day, the same thing happened: she wasn't allowed to go to her room until *after* tea, but at least she did get chance to practice again, and this time she managed to play her flute at the same time. Sometimes she hit a 'bum note', as Sam had called them, and sometimes the trumpy notes were a bit late, but she was unquestionably getting better. So she was heartbroken when, the next day, Mum told her that they wouldn't be having *any* sprouts: they'd run out, and everyone else was fed up with them, so she wouldn't be buying anymore – not for a few weeks anyway. Florence would be back at school in two days' time, and they *never* served sprouts at her school – not even at Christmas.

Would she ever play music through her bottom again?

Was her career as a flatulist over before it had begun?

Would she ever again be able to get Sam to leave the room without even having to say a word?

CHAPTER NINE

Florence spent the whole morning moping around: knowing that she couldn't have any sprouts for absolutely *ages* made her want them even more! It wasn't *fair*! But what she could she do? Then she had an idea: perhaps Grandma had some sprouts. 'Mum!' she called. 'Can I go to Grandma and Grandad's for my tea?'

'No, I don't think so,' replied Mum. 'We're going there tomorrow, for New Year's Day dinner. Had you forgotten?'

'Oh, yeah,' said Florence. 'Well, can I ring them to make sure *they* haven't forgotten as well?'

'Grandma won't have forgotten,' said Mum. 'I spoke to her yesterday and she mentioned it then.'

'Well, can I ring them anyway?' said Florence.

'I suppose so,' came the weary reply.

'OK!' Florence said happily, and picked up the phone – she lived in one of those old-fashioned houses that still used a landline for a telephone – and pressed the button that would ring her Grandma's number. As usual, Grandad answered it, because Grandma was busy doing something, and he wasn't. 'Hello, Grandad, you know we're coming for dinner tomorrow?'

'Hello, Florence. How are you?' said Grandad.

'I'm fine thank you, Grandad. *Did* you know we're coming for dinner tomorrow?' replied Florence.

'I'm very well, Florence,' said Grandad. 'Thank you for asking. And so is Grandma. In fact, she's busy in the kitchen. We're having shepherd's pie for tea.'

'With sprouts? Can I come?' said Florence.

'No, not with sprouts: with peas and carrots. Tell you what, why don't you see if you can come for dinner tomorrow?' suggested Grandad.

'We *are* Grandad! That's why I'm ringing you.' cried Florence.

'Why didn't you say so?' teased Grandad.

'I did!' said Florence. Then she paused, before asking in her best, "butter wouldn't melt in her mouth voice", 'Can you ask Grandma if she will do some... for me?'

'Some what?' asked Grandad.

'Sprouts of course!' said Florence impatiently.

Anyway, to cut a long story short, Grandma had already decided to do some sprouts, and the following day found them all sitting at Grandma and Grandad's dining table, having exactly the same things to eat as they had on Christmas Day – they even had Christmas crackers. This time though, Grandma kept a close eye on Grandad to make sure that he ate *his* sprouts himself, and didn't scrape them on to Florence's plate; but then she did give Florence quite a generous portion of her own, causing Mum to raise an eyebrow, and Sam to say, 'Hope you've got plenty of air fresheners, Grandma.'

But, to Sam's disappointment, the meal passed off without any seismic interruptions from Florence, and when no one would take up his suggestion of a game of 'Twister' – or 'Charades', he tutted, took out his mobile phone, and opened up a game to play. However, his ears pricked up when Florence asked her grandad if he'd like her to play the flute for him.

'Of course,' Grandad replied.

'Can we go in the other room then?' asked Florence.

''What on earth for?' Grandma interrupted. 'We *all* want to hear you play.'

'Yeah! Especially after last time,' Sam joined in.

'What's the matter, sweetheart?' Mum asked. 'You know we *all* love to hear you play.'

'Well, I erm...' Florence seemed lost for words, but Grandad understood instantly.

'I think,' he suggested. 'She wants to show me how she can play a duet – with herself. Have you been practising, Florence?'

Florence nodded, and it suddenly dawned on Mum. 'Of course!' she said. 'That's why you've been playing in your room every night after tea, isn't it? So that *I* didn't know you were trumping.'

Florence nodded and said, 'Sorry, Mummy.'

'And have you got better?' Dad asked.

Again Florence nodded.

'Well, that's good isn't it, Claire?' Dad said. 'She's held her trumps in all day, and then let them out in a controlled manner in private.'

'I suppose so, yes,' replied Mum.

'Right,' Grandma chimed in. 'If Claire's got even better, *I* want to hear her, and if the smell gets too bad, well, we'll just have to pinch our noses. George, open the door, let's have a bit of an air flow before we start.'

'Yeah, and turn the fire off,' said Sam. 'We don't want any explosions.'

'Ignore him,' said Grandma. 'Come on, let's hear you.'

So, while Grandad opened the door and everyone got themselves settled, Florence took out her music and her flute. She'd been practicing one of Grandma and Grandad's favourites: 'Annie's Song', which was quite easy for her to play on the flute but had quite a lot of long notes, which were much trickier to play through her bottom! As soon as Florence had played a few notes everyone was captivated, even Sam's jaw dropped open in astonishment at the purity of her trumpeting trumpy-notes, although he soon covered his mouth and nose with his hand - as did everyone else. When she'd finished, all of the adults leapt to their feet and gave her hugs of congratulations, and told her how clever she was. Sam remained seated but did admit that her performance had been, 'pretty cool'.

When they'd all finished telling each other how amazing Florence's performance had been, Grandad said, 'Well, no one can say you can't control your trumping now.'

'Pity she can't control the smell as well,' said Sam.

Mum ignored her son and said, 'Grandad's right. I *was* worried about you going back to school and... well... what would happen if you did one in your classroom, but you can obviously control them perfectly. That's brilliant. I'm not sure what your music teacher, Mrs Walker, will think though.'

'No,' agreed Dad. 'Best not play your bottom in your lessons with her – at least not without warning.'

'Can you play something else?' asked Grandad. 'Or are you out of puff, if you know what I mean?'

'I think I can,' replied Florence.' What would you like me to play?'

'How about "Candle in the Wind"?' suggested Sam.

'Yes, that would be nice,' said Grandma, before she realised what Sam had done, and added, 'Sam, don't be rude.'

'Well it does sound like a trumpet,' replied Sam. 'And that is a *wind* instrument.'

'Actually, it's brass,' Grandad corrected. 'How about "Auld Lang Syne," Florence? It is New Year's Day, after all.'

'OK,' replied his granddaughter, and she picked up her flute again and played it perfectly, even though she hadn't even practiced it as a duet with herself before.

In fact, she was so brilliant, that it gave Sam an idea; one that he couldn't tell anyone else about, at least not yet.

CHAPTER TEN

Now that Florence had proved that she could control her trumping completely, Mum was quite happy to let her have sprouts every day, although she drew the line at having them for pudding. Florence was quite happy with this arrangement, as her trumping control gave her plenty of 'puff', as Grandad had called it. Her days back at school were relatively uneventful, although she did enjoy walking past groups of children in the playground, trumping silently, and then walking away to watch them look at each accusingly when the smell became noticeable. She particularly enjoyed doing this to the Headteacher, Mrs Hughes, and the Year 6 teacher, Mrs Holmes, in the corridor. The looks of first disgust, and then embarrassment on their faces were brilliant, as they each thought the other were responsible but were too polite to say anything.

Soon, Florence was dying to show her music teacher, Mrs Walker, what she could do, but couldn't find an opportunity during school-time, so she asked her mum for help. Mum was equally keen to know the music teacher's opinion of Florence's newly-discovered talent, and she invited Mrs Walker to a private recital at their house. Of course, Grandma and Grandad were also there, as well as Mum and Dad. Sam was busy, he said, doing his homework upstairs.

Mrs Walker was used to the family recitals, because as well as being Florence's music teacher at school, she also gave her private lessons at the Foulger's house. What she wasn't used to, was Florence setting her music stand up in front of the open door and a fan blowing towards the door from the opposite side of the room. Nor was she used to being given a tissue and being told, 'You might want to use this in a minute or two.'

Then Florence began to play. There was nothing special about the first few bars but then Florence began her 'duet'. Mrs Walker immediately looked round the room to identify the trumpet player but, of course, she could find none. She couldn't understand what was going on. Florence's playing was sublime, and Mrs Walker looked round the family and smiled her appreciation at all of them, although she was puzzled to see them all holding tissues over their mouths and noses.

Then she noticed something, and immediately felt uncomfortable and looked away. The fan and the open door had done their job to some extent, but the smell was so powerful that it still permeated the living room and Mrs Walker, quite understandably, believed that one of the audience – probably Grandma or Grandad - were responsible. 'One of them must have some medical condition, and the family is bravely making the best of it,' she thought. But she couldn't bring herself to cover her own nose: she was far too polite, so she was extremely relieved when the performance finished and she could join in the enthusiastic applause with the family.

As soon as they had all finished telling Florence how wonderful she had been, Mum turned to Mrs Walker and began to explain. 'I saw you looking round for a trumpet, Debbie, but it was all Florence, although it wasn't all *flute*. The second instrument was-'

'My bottom!' Florence interrupted, since *she* wanted to be the one to tell her music teacher, because Mrs Walker was her favourite teacher. In fact, she was everyone's favourite teacher, because she was so nice and so eccentric: when she'd organised the Year 2 Nativity play at Christmas she had cast three shepherds and *nine* visitors from the east, explaining that there were 'The Three Kings',

'The Three Wise Men,' and 'The Three Magi', and that made nine altogether.

Of course, eccentric or not, Mrs Walker did not initially understand what Florence was telling her, but after Mum had explained everything, including the open door and the fan, it all became clear. And Mrs Walker, being so nice, then apologised to Grandma and Grandad for thinking one of them had been responsible for the smell. Unfortunately, she was too embarrassed to explain why she was apologising, which only added to her reputation for eccentricity. Not that anyone was worried about that: they were all too keen to know what she thought of Florence's performance and, needless to say, she thought it was absolutely amazing. The flute playing had been excellent as always, and the trumping had been completely in time and in tune. She really didn't know what to say, although she spent about ten minutes not saying it.

'Well, Florence,' she concluded. 'You have an amazing talent. I'm not sure we can use it in the school orchestra: the side effects would be rather difficult to deal with, but I must say, I would be very interested in teaching you to be even better.'

'Better? How?' asked Mum.

'Well, what Florence did this evening was to play the same thing with her flute and... her bottom. It was two instruments playing exactly the same notes. She wasn't playing it as a *duet,* where each instrument plays a different part.'

'I see, Debbie,' said Mum. Grandma and Grandad and Florence all nodded their understanding, as did Dad, although he *didn't* understand: he thought a duet was just two instruments playing the same tune. 'And you'd be interested in teaching Florence to play proper duet arrangements?'

'I certainly would,' replied Mrs Walker. 'Of course, we couldn't practice at school. Someone might come in and we don't have the ventilation in the music room to...'

'You could teach her here,' said Mum. 'You've done it before.'

'Yes, that would be fine with me,' said Mrs Walker. 'I could bring Florence home after school one evening a week, if you like, and teach her then.'

Everyone thought this was a good idea and the arrangements were made over a cup of tea – one each obviously. No one seemed to consider what Florence was going to do with her amazing new talent, but that didn't really matter, because that was precisely what Sam was working on upstairs.

CHAPTER ELEVEN

For the next two months, Mrs Walker came to the Foulger home once or twice a week; each time armed with a piece of music arranged for the flute and trumpet, and each time amazed at how wonderful Florence sounded – on *both* instruments. Mum would always join them at the end of the lesson to listen to what Florence had learnt that day, and *she* was always amazed too, although she didn't know where it would all lead. On the one hand, she was genuinely impressed and proud of how well Florence could play, but on the other, she was afraid of what people might think, if they found out that Florence was playing music by trumping and that *she*, her mother, was encouraging it. So she really didn't know what to say when, while Florence was putting her flute away upstairs after a lesson, Mrs Walker asked Mum if they were intending that Florence should perform her new skill in public.

'I'm not at all sure about that,' Mum replied. 'I mean, what would people think?

What would her friends think? They might be horrible to her, especially about the smell.'

'I know,' said Mrs Walker. 'But she really is very good. It's something to think about anyway. Have you ever discussed it with Florence?'

'No,' said Mum. 'I always thought she just wanted to play for us: that she'd find it too embarrassing to do it in public.'

'Well, it might be a good time to ask her what she wants to do, just so we all know,' said Mrs Walker.

So that evening, before Florence went to bed, Mum and Dad sat down with her in the living room, and asked her if she wanted to perform her special 'duets' in public.

'In public?' Florence said, sounding slightly frightened by the idea. 'You mean in front of people?'

'Yes,' said Mum. 'A proper audience – at school perhaps; in a concert, or an assembly.'

'In front of all my friends!' exclaimed Florence. 'They'd all laugh at me.'

'They might at first,' said Mum. 'But they'd soon stop when they heard how good you are. Sam did, remember?'

'And *he's* a boy,' Dad pointed out.

'But the... *smell*,' said Florence. 'They wouldn't like that! And then they'd make fun of me.'

Florence was clearly very upset at the idea, so Mum said, 'That's all right, darling. You don't have to. We just wanted to know if you wanted to, or not. And now we know.' Mum smiled and gave Florence a kiss and added, 'Right, time for your bath, come on. Don't think any more about it.'

After another month of twice-weekly lessons had passed (I was going to say biweekly lessons but that can also mean every two weeks rather than two times a week, and I didn't want to confuse you), Mrs Walker asked Florence's parents if she could 'have a word'. And Dad, being in his usual flippant mood, told her she could have any one she liked, as he could always get another one. And then of course, Mum asked Mrs Walker to excuse her husband and told her to carry on. So Mrs Walker, having first given Dad a "look" said, 'It's the first of May in four weeks' time.'

'It usually is at this time of year,' replied Dad.

Mum gave him a stare, told Mrs Walker to ignore him, and then said, 'And?'

'May Day!' replied Mrs Walker.

'Are you sinking?' asked an excited Dad.

'What?' asked the bemused music teacher.

'May Day! May Day!' repeated Dad. 'It's the international distress call.'

'*You'll* be internationally distressed if you don't stop messing about,' threatened Mum. 'Debbie, what about May Day?'

'We're having a May Day celebration, aren't we?' Mrs Walker explained. 'You know, dancing round the Maypole, stalls selling bric-a-brac nobody wants, face painting, throwing wet sponges at teachers.... Great fun!'

Mum held up her hand towards her husband to prevent her him saying something like, 'It sounds like as much fun as a wet Wednesday in Wolverhampton,' and replied uncertainly, 'Well... yes. I suppose we'll be there. Do we have to buy tickets? Are you selling them?'

'Oh no!' said Mrs Walker. 'You just turn up. There are no tickets, but I've been asked if the school orchestra can play, and I was wondering if Florence... er... might like to...play?'

'I'm sure she would! Of course!' Mum replied enthusiastically, until she realised what the teacher was *really* asking. 'Oh, you mean one of her "duets". No, I don't think so. Florence was quite upset at the thought of it when we asked. She's worried about how her friends would react – to the smell, obviously.'

'But they will be playing outside!' exclaimed Mrs Walker. 'Unless it's raining of course. Then we'll have to go inside and Florence could just play her flute as normal then. But if we can play outside... well, it will probably be windy – it always is at our May Day Fairs, plays havoc with the costumes and ribbons. And that would just blow any... fumes away! No one would notice a thing.'

'Oh, right. I see,' replied Mum. 'I'll have to ask her...'

'Of course!' Mrs Walker interjected.

'But to be honest,' Mum went on. 'I must warn you, I still don't think Florence will want her friends to know she's playing through her bottom. Some of them are bound to make fun of her.'

'But that's just it!' exclaimed the music teacher. 'No one has to know! We have a trumpeter in the orchestra, so everyone will just think it's him – and that he's improved a lot. I won't even tell the other members of the orchestra! If they notice anything, I'll tell them Florence has a new flute that makes a special sound.'

'Oh, I see,' said Mum. 'Well, all I can do is ask her. What do you think, Dave?' she asked her husband.

'I think... I'll get my face painted like Batman,' he replied with a big grin. 'As to Florence playing her flute at the fair, I don't see why not. Debbie's right, no one needs to know anything. It's entirely up to Florence.'

'Well, Debbie,' said Mum. 'It looks like we have Batman's approval, so I'll ask Florence tonight and let you know.'

That evening, Mum and Dad again sat down with Florence in the living room, and explained Mrs Walker's proposal, including the advantages of the orchestra playing outside. Florence took a few moments to think about it, before saying, 'So no one will smell anything?'

'No,' replied Dad. 'And even if they do, I'll tell everyone I saw a farmer spreading muck in the field at the back of the school. And they'll believe me because I'll look like Batman.'

'Never mind the bit about Batman,' Mum added. 'Daddy's right. We can always blame any smell on the farmer's muck-spreading.'

Florence thought about it again. She *did* want to play in public and see if people really liked her trumping sounds, but she didn't want them to know how she was doing it. This seemed like the perfect solution.

'I'll do it!' she said.

And so Florence's first public performance as Florence the Flute-playing Flatulist was arranged.

CHAPTER TWELVE

For Florence, the day of the May Fair came around alarmingly quickly. Not because she wasn't prepared musically, but because she was beginning to have second thoughts about playing in public. She hadn't even been able to practice her trumpeting with the orchestra, and wasn't at all sure how it would sound when she played along with the orchestra's sole trumpet player. To be honest, he wasn't very good, and it would be obvious that there were two trumpet sounds coming from the orchestra – one absolutely perfect (Florence) and one absolutely anything but perfect (little Billy Cooper). And then there was the smell: what if it *wasn't* very windy, or what if the wind suddenly dropped? Would anyone believe a word from a man who had his face painted like Batman?

But Florence needn't have worried about the wind; when the Foulger family arrived at the school it was blowing a gale – so much so that Mrs Walker was having to argue very strongly with Mrs Hughes, the Head Teacher, not to move the orchestra's performance indoors. Eventually, Mrs Hughes threw her hands up in despair, gave up, and walked away, after telling Mrs Walker that the impending orchestral disaster was all, 'down to her'.

'Everything all right?' asked Mum, when they reached Mrs Walker.

'Couldn't be better!' replied the music teacher. 'It's *very* windy – but they have clips to hold their music in position, so that should be all right. And I've *fixed* the trumpet player.'

'You've *fixed* the trumpet player!' said Dad. 'What do you mean? Have you bribed him to take a fall?'

'Ignore my husband, Debbie - again. He's been watching gangster films on the tele. But what *have* you done to Billy Cooper?'

'Nothing!' said Mrs Walker. 'Not to him, anyway. But I've stuffed something into his trumpet so that it won't make a sound, and I've told Billy that it's a special "tuning device", which will make it very difficult for him to blow, but will make his trumpet-playing sound wonderful. And I've juggled the arrangement of the orchestra, so that Florence will be standing next to Billy, and everyone will think that Florence's trumping is Billy's trumpet!'

Mrs Walker gave everyone a great big, 'haven't I done well?' smile. And Dad said, 'Haven't you done well? Where's the face painting stall?'

'Don't you dare,' said Mum. 'Sam, take your dad to find the refreshments and get me a cup of tea, will you?'

Sam, who had surprised everyone by insisting on coming to the fair (he'd previously refused to be seen 'dead' at any of his little sister's school events) held out his hand and said, 'Money?'

'That's why I said, take your dad,' replied his mum. 'And keep him away from the face painting. I don't want a repeat of the Spiderman episode.'

'That wasn't my fault!' protested Dad. 'How was I supposed to know that little boy was afraid of spiders?'

'That little boy was only three-years-old,' replied Mum. 'And what he was afraid of, was a six-foot tall spider looming over him threatening to wrap him in its web and eat him later!'

Dad shrugged his shoulders in response. 'Not my fault kids these days have no sense of humour. Come on Sam, let's see if we can clean up on the tombola.'

'Don't forget my tea!' Mum called after them, before she turned to Florence. 'Are you all right sweetheart? It sounds like Mrs Walker has arranged everything beautifully. You'll get chance to show how good you are without anyone knowing it's you, *or* how you're doing it.'

'Yes, mummy. I'm fine.' replied Florence, who did feel much better now she could see how windy it was.

'Not too late to change your mind, you know.' said Mummy.

Mrs Walker looked horrified.

'I'm fine, Mummy, really, I am.' said Florence.

'Of course you are,' said Mrs Walker. 'Come with me, Florence. It's time to start setting things up. We'll see you later, Claire.'

'Bye, Mummy!' said Florence, as she walked off with the music teacher.

'Bye, darling!' said Mummy and then thought, 'Now where's my cup of tea?' as she headed off to look for her husband and son. She went first to the face painting stall – just in case – but found Sam and his dad at the tombola. Dad was buying tickets, while Sam stood next to him, loaded up with two bottles of bubble bath, a bottle of orange squash, a packet of out-of-date biscuits, and a manicure set that looked like it had come out of a Christmas cracker.

'What *are* you two doing?' she asked.

'I'm on a roll,' replied Dad. 'I win every time – well almost. I'm after that bottle of whisky. Yes! I've won again. What is it this time?'

The woman behind the stall handed Dad his prize; a rather worn out-looking cuddly rabbit.

'Oh,' said Dad. 'Never mind, better luck next time.' Then he delved into his pockets, before looking up expectantly at his wife and asking, 'Got any change, Claire? I've run out.'

'Never mind this load of old...' Mum noticed the woman behind the stall watching and cut herself off in mid-sentence. 'What about my cup of tea?"

'Sorry, love,' replied Dad. 'Got carried away, cos' we kept winning. Got nothing left.'

'You could have a drink of orange juice if you can find a cup... and a cold water tap. *And* you could have a biscuit.' suggested Sam, not entirely helpfully.

'Save the biscuits for later,' replied Mum. 'They might be all you and your dad get for tea. Come on, let's go and get a good spot to watch Florence.'

The orchestra was setting up in a corner of the playground, which was partly sheltered from the wind by two high walls. Even here, it was still very windy, which made Florence very happy. The rest of the Foulger family managed to position themselves at the front of the gathering crowd, and Dad and Sam were soon tucking into their packet of slightly soft biscuits.

Mrs Walker gave a short introduction to the crowd, and talked about how hard the orchestra had worked, and how she hoped everyone would enjoy the performance. Then she turned her back to the audience and started waving her arms around at the orchestra, as though she were directing airborne traffic. Of course, she was really conducting the musicians and they began to play. Everything was going along quite nicely, with all the instruments being played in tune and in time. Billy Cooper was extremely pleased with how good *he* sounded. His trumpet was incredibly hard to blow, and he could feel himself going red in the face, but it was worth it because he sounded better than he ever had before. Florence, of course, was very pleased that she was able to play both her 'instruments' without anybody noticing the accompanying smell.

Unfortunately, as often happens when everything is going along so swimmingly, disaster struck, when the wind (which had been doing such a good job of dispersing the odour from Florence's trumping) suddenly decided to enjoy itself and began to swirl around in the corner of the playground like a mini-tornado. Instantly, all of the music stands were thrown to the ground, dislodging all of the clips holding the music sheets. Now the unfettered sheets of music were whirling around in the air like break-dancing butterflies. Mrs Walker carried on trying to conduct the orchestra, but none of them knew the music well enough to play it without being able to see it: none except Florence of course, who carried on playing as well as ever. Billy Cooper had stopped as well, as he was almost out of puff and hadn't a clue what notes to play anyway. This was no good to Florence, who said out of the corner of the mouth, 'Keep playing, Billy. You're doing great!'

'I can't,' Billy replied. 'I don't know the music.'

'You'll be fine,' Florence tried to reassure him, as she continued to play her flute only. 'Go on, give it a try. You might be better than you think.'

So, while the other musicians picked up their music stands, and scrambled around on the floor, leaping into the air occasionally to try to grab their sheet music, Billy put his trumpet unenthusiastically to his lips and started to blow. No one was more surprised than Billy to hear the perfect sound his trumpet appeared to be making, as he randomly pressed the valves on his instrument. He couldn't believe it! He knew *when* he should be pressing on the valves and blowing, but he hadn't a clue which valve he should be pressing, and yet it sounded absolutely perfect. Actually, there was someone who was more surprised than Billy – his parents, Mr and Mrs Cooper. They had been seriously considering hiding his trumpet and telling him that the dog must have buried it somewhere, because quite frankly, his playing was positively painful on their ears, and they'd had numerous complaints from their neighbours. But now, here was their little Billy playing better than Louis Armstrong and Miles Davis put together!

Florence and Billy eventually reached the end of the piece (Billy simply stopped playing when Florence did) and received a standing ovation from the audience, which was not surprising because there were no seats for them to sit on. The rapturous applause went on and on, and Florence and Billy, and Mrs Walker, who had been pretending to conduct them both, took bow after bow after bow. Eventually, when the applause had stopped, all of the rest of the orchestra gathered round Billy, slapping him on the back, cheering him and telling him how great he had been, leaving Florence to wander over to her parents feeling a little disappointed. She had done all of the brilliant playing of *both* instruments, but Billy Cooper was getting all of the credit. And no amount of congratulations from Mum and Dad and Mrs Walker could make her feel happy about it.

She'd suddenly realised that she *did* want people to know how good she was at playing her 'duets'.

CHAPTER THIRTEEN

That evening, Mum and Dad congratulated Florence several times on her performance, and said that she should feel very pleased and proud of herself, and Florence said that she supposed she did. But that didn't make her feel any happier. She didn't feel appreciated. How could she? No one at the fair, apart from her family and Mrs Walker, had known it was her playing the 'trumpet' so brilliantly. No one knew how difficult it was to play her flute and her bottom at the same time. No one knew how hard she had practised. And no one knew how clever she was.

Florence just couldn't see the point of playing her duets, if nobody knew she was doing it. So the next day, when her mum served up a delicious Sunday lunch of roast beef, roast potatoes, carrots, broccoli, and sprouts, Florence left her sprouts untouched at the side of her plate.

'What's the matter, darling?' asked Mum, in a worried tone. 'Are you not feeling very well?'

'I'm just fed up with sprouts, that's all' Florence replied, sulkily.

'But what about your "*trumpet* playing"?' asked Dad.

'I'm fed up with that as well,' came another sulky reply.

Mum looked at Dad, who shrugged his shoulders in a, 'I don't know either,' kind of way, and Mum knew better than to argue with Florence when she was in that sort of mood; so she cleared the plates away and said, 'I won't give you any more sprouts until you ask for them then.'

'Which will be never,' said Florence: her hatred of sprouts seeming to develop as ferociously as her love of them had. Sam looked surprised and a little disappointed with developments, but he said nothing; nothing until he found Florence in her bedroom later that afternoon, looking very bored and very fed up.

'What's up, sis?' he said, cheerily, plonking himself down on her bed next to her.

'Nothing,' she replied flatly.

'What's all this about not liking sprouts anymore then?' he asked.

'I just don't, that's all,' said Florence.

'Oh come on,' said Sam. 'You can't have gone off them that quickly. Like Dad said, what about your "*trumpeting*"?'

'I don't want to do that anymore,' Florence hissed between gritted teeth.

'But you're brilliant!' Sam exclaimed. 'Even I think so.'

'There's no point in being brilliant, if no one knows you are, and thinks someone else is playing the trumpet,' said Florence, crossly.

'Ah, so that's it,' said Sam. 'You're cross because everyone thought that Billy Cooper was playing *his* trumpet brilliantly, and didn't know it was you.'

'Yes,' replied Florence, her bottom lip sticking out so far an elephant could have perched on it.

'W...e...ll,' said Sam. 'What would you say if I told you I could do something about that? In fact, that I already have?'

'What? What do mean?' said Florence, her bottom lip now back where it belonged.

'Well, don't tell Mum yet,' Sam replied, lowering his voice and then explaining everything to his little sister, who listened with her eyes and mouth wide-open. When he'd finished he repeated, 'Don't tell Mum, OK? We should receive an email this week confirming everything, and then it'll be too late for her to stop it.'

'OK,' said Florence. 'Are you sure I'll get in? I mean what about the... smell?'

'All sorted. Don't you worry about that,' replied Sam. 'Don't forget, don't say a word to Mum... or Dad.'

So Florence said nothing to anybody about what Sam had told her, and she spent the next couple of days waiting for the email to arrive, wondering what would happen when it did, and trying (and failing) to act normally in front of her parents. Mum became convinced Florence was developing some sort of nervous condition and kept making a fuss of her daughter; whereas Dad became convinced *Mum* was developing some sort of nervous condition, because of the way she was fussing over Florence.

It was not until the following Thursday evening that all of the nervous tension in the Foulger household was suddenly released. Dinner was 'in the oven', Florence was watching television, Dad was reading the paper, Sam was just coming downstairs, (having got home late after football practice) when Mum came out of the kitchen and announced, 'D'you know? I've not looked at my emails for ages! I've probably got an inbox full of rubbish. I think I'll check it while the dinner's cooking. Where's the laptop Dave?'

'Where it always is... in Sam's room,' came the reply.

Mum turned in the doorway of the living room and said to Sam, who had just reached the bottom of the stairs, 'Be a darling and just pop back upstairs and bring me the laptop, will you?'

'What for?' asked Sam, almost accusingly.

'So that I can check my emails. I haven't done it for months,' said Mum.

'I can do that for you,' said Sam. 'No need for you to bother with it. Probably all spam anyway.'

'But there *might* be something interesting,' said Mum. 'You never know. And anyway, you don't know my password, do you?'

'Oh, er... no, I don't,' fibbed Sam.

'So go and get it, will you?" Mum insisted.

'Yes, OK! OK!' said Sam, turning reluctantly upstairs and returning a minute later with the laptop.

Mum sat next to her husband on the sofa, opened up the laptop, switched it on, and waited a few minutes while it 'logged her on'. Sam looked nervously at Florence, but she was completely engrossed in her television programme, leaving her brother to worry on his own.

'Good god,' said Mum. 'Look at this lot. I've got a screen-full of unread emails. Right, let's see what I can get rid of. That's rubbish: delete. That's rubbish: delete.'

'Are you going to give us all a running commentary on the deleting of your emails?' moaned Dad. 'I'm trying to read the paper.'

'Terribly *sorry*!' said Mum, sarcastically. 'Something important in your comic today, is there? *I'll* be quiet... Hello, what's this?'

'If you're still looking at your Inbox, it's probably an email,' said Dad. 'I thought you were going to be quiet.'

'There's one here from "Now, You're A Star!",' explained a puzzled Mum.

'And have you entered it?' asked Dad, not noticing Florence's head spin round at the mention of the TV programme.

'Of course not,' replied Mum.

'Then it's probably a scam or a virus or something,' said Dad. 'Better not open it, just delete it.'

'Oops! Too late, I've opened it,' said Mum. 'So, it says, "Congratulations! You're in! You're on your way to being a star!" What on earth is this all about, Dave?'

'Don't ask me,' replied Dad. 'I told you to delete it. You've probably infected the laptop with a virus now! Cost me a fortune to get it fixed.'

Mum ignored her husband; there was something about Sam's complete silence, and the excitement on Florence's face, that told her this was no scam email. 'Sam, what do *you* know about this?'

'It's not a scam!' Sam blurted out. 'But it's not for you... or me! It's for Florence. She's been accepted on "Now You're a Star!", playing her duets. She's *bound* to win!'

'Florence, did you know about this?' asked Mum.

Her daughter was too shocked and excited *and* nervous to answer, so Sam jumped in again, babbling, 'I told her on Sunday, when she was feeling fed up. And it's a good job I did, because she was fed up because Billy Cooper got all the credit for her "trumpeting" and no one realised how good she is, and now they'll all find out when she's on the show, and she'll win it as well!'

'You silly boy! Florence doesn't want to stand up in front of millions of people on the television and let them know that she plays tunes through her bottom, do you, Florence?' said Mum.

Florence was still only capable of nodding, so that's what she did.

'*Really*?' said Mum. 'But what about what your friends will think? I thought you said you'd be too embarrassed to show them what you can do.'

'She was,' Sam butted in. 'But she was so fed up that Billy Cooper got all the credit that she wants people to know now!'

Mum looked at Florence, 'Is this true, darling?'

Florence nodded once more, and before Mum could say anything else, Sam jumped in again, 'And before you say anything about the

100

smell, they said their theatres have huge air-conditioning systems that can deal with anything, so that won't be a problem.'

Mum shook her head in disbelief. 'Are you *sure* about this Florence?'

'Yes, Mummy,' replied Florence, having got her voice back at last. 'I want people to know how good I am. It's not fair that Billy Cooper got all the credit. And Sam says it's nothing to be ashamed of. There've been lots of people who could do it, but Sam says none of them were as good as me.'

'Well, they *probably* weren't,' said Sam.

'Dave, can't you say something?' Mum demanded.

Dad fought the impulse to ask how long dinner would be and replied, 'Look, if it's what Florence wants, then why not? We'll have to get reassurances from the TV Company about stuff, but I don't see a problem. Florence *is* brilliant, after all. And there are some good prizes on that programme, and it'd be good if another flaming dog act didn't win.'

'Hmm,' said Mum. 'I don't know. We'll have to think about it later. In the meantime Sam, you can tell me how you've managed to do all of this through my email system, if you *didn't* know my password.'

CHAPTER FOURTEEN

So that evening, Mum and Dad discussed Florence's taking part in the show, while Florence lay awake in bed worrying about it.

Mum wasn't convinced that Florence really wanted to do it and Dad said, 'Well, she *said* she wants to.' And Mum said she knew that, but wasn't sure if Sam had persuaded her. And then Dad said, 'Well, he said he didn't. He said she was very keen on the idea.' And Mum said she knew that as well. And then there was a lot more of Mum expressing her doubts, and Dad repeating what Florence and Sam had said, and Mum saying that she knew *that* as well.

Having got nowhere with that sort of discussion, Mum and Dad started talking about the ramifications (in other words what would happen) if Florence did do the show. Dad pointed out that the prizes were good – lots of money and no doubt a recording contract, and Florence would be famous. Mum pointed out that Florence hadn't won yet, and that she would be very famous after the first live audition, and that being famous for a ten-year-old girl wasn't necessarily a good thing. Even if she didn't do very well, the newspapers and the television companies would be very interested in a little girl who could play tunes through her bottom. They'd be queueing up outside the house. The family would get no privacy. Dad suggested that he could become Florence's manager and organise the 'Press'. Mum pointed out that he couldn't organise alcoholic refreshment in a brewery – or words to that effect.

Although they carried on debating the pros and cons of Florence taking part in the TV show all evening, all they concluded was that they should leave it up to Florence to decide: if she still wanted to do it in the morning, then she could.

That night, although Florence fell asleep worrying about playing her bottom on television (What if she couldn't do it on the night? What would her friends think? What would her teachers think? Would everyone make fun of her?) she had an absolutely fantastic dream, in which she won the show, and everyone absolutely loved her trumpeting, and even loved the smell, which became a best-selling perfume called 'Parfum du Florence', produced by Victoria Beckham! So it should come as no surprise to you, although it did to her mum and dad, that the following morning she was extremely excited about being on the TV show, and asked if she could have her special sprout muesli and sprout smoothie for breakfast.

Mrs Walker was almost as excited as Florence when Mum told her about Florence being in "Now You're A Star!" 'Right,' she said. 'We'll have to tell Mrs Hughes, to warn her that her school could be getting some publicity.'

'Will she mind?' asked Mum.

'Oh no!' replied Mrs Walker. 'It'll only be good publicity because Florence is so good. And I suppose we'll have to explain everything to the rest of the children – especially Billy Cooper: he thinks he's suddenly become a great trumpet player. Oh! And we'll have to decide what music Florence is going to play. Does she have any ideas?'

'I don't know,' replied Mum. 'I've not asked her yet.'

'Right, well, I'm her music teacher, I suppose I should have some ideas. I'll go away and think about it,' said Mrs Walker. 'Gosh it's so exciting.' And with that she was off!

Mrs Walker had a harder time than she'd anticipated, persuading Mrs Hughes that it would be good for the school if Florence was seen on TV playing 'flute and bottom' duets. However, when Mrs Hughes heard Florence play for her and the rest of Florence's class, she was totally won over. (Mrs Walker made sure the headteacher was standing by an open window.) All of Florence's classmates were amazed and gave her a huge round of applause. Nobody at all laughed, in fact, a lot of them, mainly boys, thought the smell was absolutely hilarious - even though they could hardly breathe.

The most surprising reaction came from Billy Cooper who, far from being disappointed that it hadn't been him who sounded so good at the school fair, was actually relieved. He'd tried playing the trumpet since, but had been as bad ever and couldn't understand it. Billy's dad thought he was doing it on purpose so that he'd be able to give up playing the trumpet and play more football instead. He couldn't wait to get home and explain everything to his parents!

Now that Florence's teachers and friends knew about Florence's special talent and were supporting her, the next few weeks went by very smoothly. The only thing Florence had to put up with was her friends repeatedly asking her if she could show them how to 'play' their bottoms. But no matter how often she showed them, none of them could do it. Some of them even started eating ridiculous amounts of sprouts, but all that did was create incredibly, horrendously, obnoxious smells in the classroom, so much so that their class teacher, Mrs Wilkinson, had to send a note home with all of the children asking their parents not to feed them so many sprouts!

Mrs Walker came to the Foulgers' house almost every evening to help Florence practice, and the whole family was so excited that they encouraged her to practice almost every waking hour. In fact, Florence practiced so often that the Foulgers and Mrs Walker all became desensitized to the smell (which means they didn't notice it any more) and didn't bother to open the windows. But something must have escaped from the house, because whenever any dog-walkers went past they found themselves suddenly dragged to the opposite side of the road by their dogs, who were trying to escape the obnoxious odours. Of course, keeping the windows closed had the unfortunate effect of the noxious gases building up inside the house, so that when Mum opened the front door to the window cleaner, who only wanted to collect his money, the gas rolled out of the door, enveloping the poor man and he collapsed in a heap on the floor. Mum helped him back to his car, telling him that his vertigo must be playing up again (which is an unfortunate condition for someone who spends most of the day up a ladder).

Soon the time came for the first show; the first round of the competition. And Florence was ready; the question was: were the judges?

CHAPTER FIFTEEN

The day of the first round of the TV competition finally arrived. There were to be three rounds in all: this preliminary round, a 'semi-final' and then the 'Grand Final'. The first round was taking place in a large theatre in Manchester, which was quite convenient for Florence and her family as they all lived in Stockport, and could easily catch the train into the city.

The whole family, together with Mrs Walker, travelled into Manchester. But while Grandma and Grandad, Sam, and Mrs Walker could go and find somewhere to have something to eat, Florence, with Mum and Dad, had to go to the theatre to register and be told what to do.

After she'd registered and had had everything explained, Florence and her parents were told to go and wait 'backstage' in a huge room, with all of the other competitors and *their* families and friends. While she was waiting, Florence felt very nervous, and so did Mum and Dad. They could watch the acts that were on before Florence on an enormous screen on the wall, and see the huge audience clapping and cheering if they liked what they were watching, or booing if they didn't - or didn't like one of the judge's comments. Some of the other competitors joined in with the cheering and booing, but Florence was far too nervous to do that.

After every act they saw, Dad told Florence that she was better than them so she had nothing to worry about. Of course, this didn't stop Florence worrying: in fact, it made it worse, as she began to think that she'd let everyone down if she didn't perform very well. She fidgeted with her flute, picking it up and putting it down; kept messing with her hair, which was in bunches, which she didn't like anymore, but Dad had said that it made her look sweet, and would get the two female judges on her side as soon as she walked out on stage. When Mum told her to stop messing with her hair (as she'd ruin it) Florence began to fiddle with the hem of her dress, which again she didn't like – it was covered in tiny flowers – but again, Dad had said it made her look sweet. Eventually, Mum told Dad to be quiet, and she held Florence's hand to stop her fidgeting.

Florence looked around the room at the other contestants, and saw an amazing array of costumes: one old man was dressed as a chicken; another seemed to be covered in fairy-lights; there was a large group of girls dressed in sparkly leotards; a few ladies were wearing posh long dresses; a large group of men, a little bit older than Dad, were all wearing smart black suits and bowties; although a lot of the younger contestants were dressed quite casually in jeans. Some of the others were older than her Grandma and Grandad, including the man dressed as a chicken; some were about the same age as Mum and Dad, one or two looked to be the same age as Florence, but most of them looked like they'd just left school or university. Florence wanted to have a quick practice like some of the others were – playing guitars, juggling chain saws or just singing – but she didn't think anyone would like it if she started to practice her 'trumpeting'. And anyway, she needed to save her 'puff'.

Finally, a young man dressed in a crumpled t-shirt and jeans, wearing a microphone headset (on his head of course) appeared, and told Florence it was her turn next. Florence and Mum and Dad followed the man to the 'wings' at the side of the stage. There, the man in the crumpled t-shirt said quietly, 'You're the one playing the "duet", aren't you?'

Florence nodded.

'Great! It sounds brilliant. The judges will love it. And don't worry about the... side effects, I've already turned the air-con up to maximum, so no one will smell a thing!' That made Florence feel a bit better, but before she could say anything there was a huge round of applause as the previous act left the stage, and the man was saying, 'Right, it's your turn Florence, off you go. Good luck!'

Mum grabbed Florence quickly, gave her a kiss and said, 'Don't worry, sweetheart, you'll be brilliant. Good luck!'

'Yes, good luck, darling,' said Dad, also giving Florence a kiss, and then as she started to walk out on stage he shouted, 'Break a leg!'

Florence looked back at him, confused, which made her look even more nervous than she actually was. Why did her daddy want her to break a leg? She thought he wanted her to win! The four judges sitting just in front of the stage watched as she walked uncertainly towards the centre of the stage, where there were two microphones set up at just the right heights for her - one at head height and one at... bottom height!

Both of the female judges, Amelia and Nina, were smiling at each other and saying,

'She's so sweet!' One of them even had a tear in her eye, as the head judge, Nigel Barlow, who was something to do with the music industry and was often very nasty to the contestants, looked at Florence, smiled, and said, 'Hello sweetheart, what's your name?'

'Florence,' came the almost inaudible reply.

'Can you speak up please?' said the judge. 'I can hardly hear you. There's no need to be nervous.'

Of course, Florence didn't believe that at all and coughed nervously, before repeating her name more loudly.

'Florence? That's a nice name,' said the judge. 'And how old are you, Florence?'

'Ten,' said Florence, 'and a half.'

There was a big 'Ah' from the audience, and the two female judges smiled at each other again and silently mouthed, 'So sweet!'

'And what are you going to do for us today, Florence?' asked Nigel.

Florence held up her flute and said, 'I'm going to play a duet.'

All of the judges exchanged puzzled glances, before the other male judge, Hughie, who hadn't done anything other than be a judge on talent shows for so long that no one could remember what he'd done before, asked, 'How are you going to do that Florence? A duet needs two people, doesn't it? I can see two microphones, although one is very low and there's only one of you.'

'My daddy says I have to tell you to wait and see,' Florence replied, and was surprised by the sound of laughter filling the theatre and the sight of the judges chuckling, as she hadn't said anything funny.

Then Hughie replied, 'Well, I suppose you'd better do what your daddy says.'

'He told me to break a leg when I came out!' said Florence. 'But I don't want to do that.'

Again she was puzzled by the laughter from the audience and the judges, until one of the female judges - the one with the long blonde hair and the black sparkly dress, not the one with the long dark hair and the silver sparkly dress - explained, 'Oh, sweetheart, that means "good luck" in the theatre. So he wasn't being nasty.'

The head judge, Nigel, then said, 'Right, Florence, take your time. When you're ready, off you go. Let's hear your *"duet"*.'

This was it! Florence lifted her flute to her lips, and the audience fell silent as she took a deep breath and began to play.

CHAPTER SIXTEEN

Having expected Florence to play a beautiful, slow piece of music, the audience and judges were astonished to hear her launch into the William Tell Overture (which is an extremely *fast* piece of music) especially when it started with a trumpet! Almost everyone in the theatre instantly leapt to their feet and started cheering. The judges were laughing, but were obviously confused as they looked around, trying to see who was playing the trumpet.

Florence finally put her flute to her lips and began to play that as well. The audience cheered even louder. They all recognised the music, although not very many of them knew what it was called, and Grandad shouting, 'Hi Ho Silver! Away!' didn't help much. Soon the four judges were on their feet and bouncing along to the music; Hughie was pretending to ride a galloping horse, and that was when it happened. That was when the two female judges, Amelia and Nina, started to look accusingly at Nigel and Hughie, *and* when Nigel and Hughie started shrugging their shoulders in wide-eyed innocence. There was a definite smell, and all of the judges were denying responsibility for it. And it was getting stronger... and stronger. The judges put tissues to their noses, as the audience in the first few rows behind them also started to notice the rather unpleasant odour. A wave of reaction spread back through the vast auditorium row by row, as the smell rolled out over the audience; everyone looking at everyone else in the same accusing manner. Many of the audience started to laugh about the smell, especially the boys, but they all carried on cheering the amazing musician on stage – in between coughing and spluttering.

Florence was totally oblivious to what was happening, as she'd closed her eyes in an effort to concentrate on her music and forget about how many people were watching her. When she finished, the audience cheered and applauded thunderously. The judges, still on their feet, tried to combine enthusiastic applause with covering their noses, and when Florence saw their tissues she knew that the air conditioning had not been entirely successful, and she smiled nervously.

The judges sat down, as did the audience, and Nigel, the head judge said, 'That was absolutely brilliant, Florence. You played so beautifully. And how you got your flute to sound like a trumpet is utterly beyond me. But I must apologise for the *terrible* smell. There must be something wrong with the drains. I'm surprised it didn't put you off.'

'That was me,' said Florence quietly. 'I'm sorry.'

'Pardon?' said Nigel. 'Can you speak up again, Florence? The audience are coughing and laughing too much. I think the smell has reached *them*.'

'That was me,' said Florence more clearly. 'The smell... it was me.'

'No, Florence,' said Nigel. 'It can't have been you. A sweet little ten-year-old girl cannot possibly make a smell as noxious as that *and* fill the whole theatre with it.'

'No, really it *was* me,' insisted Florence, thinking honesty was the best policy. 'That's how I play the trumpet at the same time as the flute. I... I'm a flatulist.'

'A what?' asked Hughie.

'A flatulist,' repeated Florence. 'I can play tunes through my bottom.'

The whole audience erupted in raucous laughter, as did the judges - once what Florence had said had sunk in. The sound of the laughter and the fact that it seemed to be aimed at her began to upset Florence, but Mum was watching closely and she marched on to the stage and put her arm round Florence. 'Don't worry, darling,' she said. 'You were brilliant; absolutely brilliant!'

Mum's presence on stage seemed to calm the judges and they all stopped laughing. 'I hope you've finished laughing at my daughter now,' said Mum, scowling down at the embarrassed judges.

'I'm sorry,' said Nigel, smiling uncertainly. 'That was very rude of us. But you must realise that we weren't laughing at you, Florence, we were laughing at... well we were laughing that anyone could do a trump and make such a beautiful sound, and a smell that could fill the whole theatre; *and* you're only ten years old!' He looked at Mum. 'So you must be "Mum",' he added. 'You have an exceptionally gifted daughter.'

'I know,' replied Mum. 'She's brilliant.'

The smell had begun to clear by now, as Florence was no longer playing the 'trumpet' and the air conditioning was feeding in fresh air.

'How long have you been a ...' began Nigel, before forgetting the word he was looking for.

'Flatulist,' said Florence, her voice sounding a lot more confident now she had Mum with her. 'Since I found out that I absolutely love sprouts last Christmas.'

'Sprouts?' said Nigel. 'Your... *gift* comes from your love of sprouts?'

'And being a brilliant musician,' interrupted Mum.

'Yes,' said Florence, ignoring her Mum. 'I used to hate sprouts, but last Christmas I found out that I actually love them, and now I eat them all the time. I've even had them with custard!'

The audience went 'Urgh!' and Nigel said, '*Custard*?'

'Yes,' replied Florence, now full of confidence. 'I can eat sprouts with anything, but they fill me with wind, and I have to let it out, and then I found that I can control my trumps and play tunes with them.'

'You can certainly do that,' said Hughie. 'And you definitely made that tune your own. And to think I thought a flatulist was someone who came from "Flatuland"! What do you think girls?'

'You were absolutely brilliant!' said Nina. 'And I love your dress. You look so lovely!'

119

'Yes, you do,' agreed Amelia. 'Those bunches are *so* sweet. And your playing of both "*instruments*" was absolutely perfect. Such a beautiful tone and on time, all the way through. I honestly thought there was someone in the wings playing the trumpet.'

'Well,' said Nigel. 'I'd like to talk to you all day but we have other acts to see. I think we're all in agreement, do you want to start us off, Hughie?'

'Definitely,' replied Hughie. 'Florence, Now-'

'You're-' said Nina.

'A-' added Amelia.

'Star!' finished Nigel. 'That's it. We'll see you in the semi-final, Florence. Thank you for coming in and making my day.'

The audience rose to their feet once more as Florence and Mum left the stage, where Dad gave them both a big hug and they met Daniel O'Bleary, the presenter of the show, who asked Florence all about sprouts and trumping again. He couldn't keep them chatting for too long however, as he had other acts to talk to as well, so Florence, and Mum and Dad were soon in a restaurant with Grandma, Grandad, Sam, and Mrs Walker, having a celebratory meal in the city centre, which of course, had to include sprouts.

CHAPTER SEVENTEEN

As with all of the preliminary rounds of 'Now You're A Star!', the show Florence had appeared in was recorded, and was not seen on television until several weeks later; and it was only then that she became famous. Suddenly, all of the newspapers and television channels wanted to talk to her, and of course, for her to play for them. Fortunately, Mum and Dad had given a lot of thought to this, and had taken advice from the people who produced 'Now You're A Star!'. They allowed only the television channel that showed the programme to interview her, and told all of the newspaper people to watch the interview on television. So that's what the journalists did, before writing their own articles and headlines based on it. Florence's favourite headline was, 'Fantastic Florence Foulger, the Flatulistic Flautist!'

Naturally, Florence was even more popular at school having done so well on the show, and was besieged with requests for her to play something – even without her flute. Some even asked her to play at their birthday parties. Mrs Walker, who was especially pleased, carried on visiting the Foulger household several times a week, to help Florence practice for the semi-final show in a few weeks' time.

Things were all going very well; Mrs Walker was happy with Florence's progress in learning her piece for the semi-final; the newspapers weren't bothering them; the family were still desensitised to the smell and didn't mind Florence practicing with the windows closed; and everyone was getting lots of iron - because they were having sprouts with every meal.

Then the telephone rang.

It was the producer of 'Now You're A Star!'.

There was a problem.

With Florence, or rather her trumping.

Someone in 'Health and Safety' had said that the smell was unacceptable. That it must be unhealthy. It could even be a fire hazard. They were very sorry, but they could not allow Florence to take part in the semi-final.

Florence was heart-broken. She pushed her sprouts away, untouched.

In fact, the whole family pushed their sprouts away, untouched. They were all heartbroken. Even the pet hamster looked miserable. Only a week to go and Florence's dreams had been crushed. Mum and Dad tried to console her: at least everyone knew how good she was now, and she'd done wonders for the country's sprout-growing farmers. But Florence didn't really care about the sprout-growing farmers – she didn't really care about sprouts anymore. She was inconsolable, and so Dad made a rather rash promise. 'Don't worry, Florence,' he said. 'I'll sort something out. You'll be able to play in the semi-final, I promise.'

Florence's eyes lit up with joy, until she saw that familiar look in Mum's eyes. Dad was talking rubbish. He couldn't sort it out. But she said, 'Thanks, Dad. But there's nothing we can do.' And then she slunk off to bed.

'What did you have to say a stupid thing like that for?' hissed Mum, as soon as Florence had left the room. 'Getting her hopes up like that!'

'I just couldn't stand seeing her so upset,' replied Dad. 'There must be *something* we can do.'

'What then, Einstein? You're the genius who's going to sort it, are you?' said Mum.

Dad sighed. 'Probably not,' he said. 'But I'm going to try to think of something.'

Mum gave a 'Humph', and said, 'Well, I won't hold my breath,' before going upstairs to try to cheer Florence up before she went to sleep.

She came downstairs to find her husband on the phone. 'And you can do that?' he was saying. 'You can test it and prove it's safe?'

The reply was obviously a 'Yes,' because Dad said, 'That's great. See you tomorrow after school. You know where we are...? Right, see you then.'

'Who was that?' asked Mum. 'Who's going to see who?'

'Krish Narayan, Sam's chemistry teacher,' replied Dad. 'He reckons he can prove Florence's trumps are not toxic and not flammable. He's coming round tomorrow to do some tests to prove it.'

'And you thought of that all by yourself?' said an astonished Mum.

'It wasn't difficult,' said Dad, rather immodestly. 'They gave the reasons why Florence couldn't play in the semi-final, but they were clearly only someone's opinions:

"must be unhealthy"; "may be flammable". Nobody knows for definite, so I thought maybe someone could do some tests to prove it, one way or the other. And I thought of Sam's chemistry teacher.'

'O-M-G,' said Mum. 'I'm married to a genius. Hang on, you said nobody knows for definite, so the tests might prove the show's "Health and Safety" right.'

'Krish said that's extremely unlikely,' replied Dad. 'He's confident he'll be able to give Florence's trumps the all clear tomorrow.'

So the following evening Sam's chemistry teacher, Mr Narayan arrived at the Foulgers' house just in time for tea, and they all sat down to a lovely roast beef dinner with copious amounts of sprouts. Unfortunately, Mum had forgotten that Mr Narayan was a vegetarian, but he said that was all right - he would simply not have any beef or gravy. He did however, ask if he could see Florence eat sprouts and custard for pudding, as he couldn't imagine such a cocktail of food being edible. Of course, Florence was only too happy to oblige, as the chemistry teacher had already assured her that his tests would prove her trumps to be harmless, and she wanted to eat as many sprouts as possible, so that she could start practicing again later that evening.

After they'd eaten, they all went into the living room and Mr Narayan brought in a very expensive-looking piece of equipment.

'Blimey!' gasped Dad. 'What's that? You nicked it from NASA?'

Krish looked at Dad and realised that Dad wouldn't understand the science behind the equipment, so he replied, 'It's just a portable gas monitor. Works on chromatography. I'll hold this sampling device in the air and start the pump and that will suck Florence's trumps through the machine and it'll tell us what's in them. Right Florence, would you care to provide a sample?'

'Shall I play the flute at the same time?' she asked.

'Oh, yes please,' replied the chemistry teacher. 'I'm ashamed to say that I missed your first performance on the show.'

So Florence picked up her flute and launched into The William Tell Overture again. Mr Narayan was enraptured: he couldn't believe how authentic the trumpet sounded, and the flute playing was sublime. He was completely lost in the music and had forgotten why he was there – until the incredible smell slapped him in the face and his eyes began to water.

'Agh!' he spluttered. 'Of course, the sample!' He started the pump and watched his machine as Dad handed him a tissue which he used to cover his nose. 'That should be enough,' he gasped after a few seconds. 'Just take a minute for the machine to churn out the results.'

Florence stopped playing and Dad asked the chemistry teacher if he'd like to step outside for a breath of fresh air. Mr Narayan accepted the offer eagerly and he and Dad went out into the back garden. He stood still for a few moments drawing in huge breaths of sweet-smelling fresh air and then said, 'The smell – it didn't seem to bother you or your family?'

'No, we've become desensitized to it,' explained Dad. 'Not bothered us for a while.'

'I see,' said Mr Narayan. 'That's just as well, I suppose.' He looked at his watch and added, 'Right, results should be ready. Let's go and have a look, shall we?'

Dad lead the way back into the living room and Mr Narayan walked over to his machine and said, 'Yes, all done,' as he ripped a short printout off the equipment. He showed this to Mum and Dad, who looked at it, and him, blankly. The teacher smiled, he'd seen exactly the same blank look on their son's face often. 'It's fine,' he said. 'A bit of methane and a few other organics, some sulphur compounds to give you that special aroma, but nothing in sufficient concentration to present a health hazard. I'm happy to tell you that Florence's trumps are perfectly safe.'

'Thank goodness for that,' said Mum. 'But what about the flammability risk?'

'Oh, I can see from the read out that it's not flammable either.'

'Shouldn't we test it to make sure?' asked Dad. 'Light a match or something? I've heard that people do set light to them; burn their bottoms sometimes as well.'

'Certainly do!' butted in Sam.

'And how would *you* know?' Mum challenged.

'Oh, just heard, that's all – like Dad,' Sam replied, unconvincingly.

'That's the point,' said the chemistry teacher. 'You have to set light to trumps at the source – where the concentration of flammable gasses is high enough. They get too dilute as they disperse into a large room.'

'Of course! Krish is right!' exclaimed Dad. 'We already know Florence's trumps are not flammable in a large room.'

'Do we?' said Mum.

'Yes!' said Dad. 'Don't forget, we've been listening to Florence practicing over the last few weeks with the windows closed and the fire on; and you've even lit candles; and we're all still here to tell the tale.'

'That's true,' said Mum. 'Well, thanks Krish, you *and* my husband have solved our problem. Would you like to hear Florence play again? I'm sure she has plenty of non-toxic wind left.'

'Oh, er, no thank you,' replied Mr Narayan. 'I must be going. I'll make sure I watch the semi-final though.' And with that, the chemistry teacher left, and the Foulger family spent the rest of the evening congratulating Dad on thinking of testing the trumps in the first place.

The next morning, Mum rang the show's producer to give her the good news, and she too was very pleased, because Florence was already 'the nation's favourite', and the television company would have been very unpopular if it had not allowed her to compete.

Their joy lasted two hours. That was when the producer rang back and informed them that the other contestants in Florence's semi-final were complaining that the smell from Florence's trumps would put them off. They were all refusing to take part if Florence was in the show. And with no contestants there could be no show

Florence still couldn't compete in the semi-final.

CHAPTER EIGHTEEN

'What now, Einstein?' Mum said, looking at her husband. 'Any more bright ideas? How are we going to stop Florence's trumps smelling?'

'Feed her something else?' suggested Dad. 'Or add something sweet-smelling to her sprouts? I mean trumps don't always smell the same, do they? So different foods must cause different smells. We just have to find one that makes nice-smelling trumps.'

'And get Florence to eat it! And anyway, if there was such a thing, I think everyone would already know about it.' said Mum.

'That's true,' said Dad. 'In that case, I don't know what we can do - apart from break the news as gently as we can when Florence gets back from school. I've got to get going, I'll see you later.' He kissed his wife on the cheek and left for work, leaving Mum wondering how on earth she could break the news to her daughter.

That evening, Mrs Walker brought Florence home so that they could practice her piece for the semi-final. Mum said nothing until they'd finished practising, but then she asked them both to sit down because, 'she had something to tell them'. 'It's about the semi-final,' she said. She paused, took a deep breath and then went on. 'The people from the programme rang yesterday and told us that Florence couldn't be in it, because Health and Safety had said...'

'Oh yes!' interrupted Mrs Walker. 'Florence told me. They said her trumps might be poisonous or catch fire, but Sam's chemistry teacher proved that that's not true, so everything's all right.'

'Well, yes he did,' replied Mum. 'But no, it isn't.'

'Isn't what?' asked Mrs Walker.

'Isn't all right,' said Mum. 'You see...'

She was interrupted by the front door opening and her husband calling, 'Hello, everyone. I've got some good news, Daddy's done it again!' He came into the living room with a great big, beaming smile on his face. 'I've solved our problem... well, probably.'

'What problem?' asked Florence and Mrs Walker, together.

'You've not told them yet?' said Dad, looking at Mum.

'I was just about to,' replied Mum. 'So how have you *probably* solved the problem?'

'*What problem?*' asked Florence and Mrs Walker, again in perfect harmony.

'Oh,' replied Mum. 'After I'd rung the producer to tell her that your trumps are not toxic and won't catch fire, she rang me back to say that the other contestants were complaining about the smell anyway, and that you still can't compete.'

'What?' shouted Florence, her eyes filling up instantly.

'It's all right! It's all right!' said Dad. 'I think I've found a solution.'

'Go on then,' said Mum. 'If you've solved this one, I'll start to believe I really have married a genius.'

'Right,' said Dad. 'Well you know how we were talking about changing the smell of the trumps, by getting Florence to eat something that made them smell nice?'

'Yes,' said Mum, exaggerating her patient tone of voice. 'But we decided that there's no such thing.'

'No, probably not,' said Dad. 'But changing the smell is still the only thing we can try to do, isn't it? And if we can't change the smell *before* Florence trumps, then we'll have to change it *after* she trumps.'

'I'm sorry,' said Mum. 'You've lost me.'

'And me,' said Mrs Walker.

'It's simple,' explained Dad. 'We add something to the air around Florence that smells really nice and covers up the smell of the trumps. Nobody can complain about a nice smell, can they?'

'No, but how do we do that?' asked Mum, still trying to sound more patient than she felt.

'Well,' replied Dad. 'I remembered today, how the sewage works near where I grew up sometimes used to smell really nice.'

'Did it?' said Mum. 'You sure you weren't having a funny dream again?'

'Quite sure,' said Dad. 'I remember asking my dad why sewage smelled nice sometimes. And he said it was because they sprayed a sort of perfume into the air to mask the horrible smells.'

'Did they?' said a somewhat disbelieving Mum.

'Yes!' said Dad, a little exasperated by his wife's scepticism. 'He showed me once. They had tall poles spaced around the boundary fence with nozzles on the top. And when the wind was blowing towards the houses they'd spray perfume out to cover up the smell of the sewage.'

'And you think we could do that to cover up the smell of Florence's trumps?' said Mum.

'Yes, why not?' replied Dad. 'I rang up the water company this afternoon, and then I went to the old sewage works to have a look at the equipment. It's all manky and rusty now but I had a good look at it, and then I went back to the office and made some sketches of what we need. Then I went down to the factory and got a couple of the lads to knock them up. We should be OK with one pole at each side of the stage spraying out the perfume while Florence is playing. Then I rang the producer of the show and she agreed that we can do a trial the day after tomorrow to see if it works. Oh! Florence will have to have the day off school. Do you think that will be OK, Debbie?'

'I'm sure it will be,' replied Mrs Walker. 'The head is very enthusiastic about Florence's TV appearances.'

'Well,' said Mum. 'It looks like I really have married a genius. What do you think, Florence?'

Florence leapt up off the sofa and threw herself into Dad's arms. 'Thank you, thank you, Daddy,' she said. 'You are so clever!'

Two days later, Mum, Dad, Florence, and Mrs Walker, as well as three men from where Dad worked, turned up at the theatre for the perfume-spraying trials. The three men got to work immediately, setting up the poles with the nozzles on the top at each side of the stage, and running a small pipe from them to a big tank of perfume, which they installed behind the curtains at the back of the stage. While all that was going on Mum, Dad, Florence, and Mrs Walker chatted to the producer of the show, a tall slim lady with very short dark hair, dressed in skinny black jeans and a black t-shirt with a big sparkly star on it. She told them how pleased everyone was that Florence's dad had come up with a solution. The people who ran the television channel were all really keen that Florence should play in the semi-final.

Once all the equipment was ready, Florence took her place on the stage, Dad went over to the perfume pump by the tank, and Mum, Mrs Walker, and the producer, as well as the men from Dad's company, spread themselves around in the theatre seats. Then Dad started the pump and adjusted it until a fine mist was being emitted from the top of the poles, and then Florence started to play her 'trumpet'.

As usual, it sounded amazing, but no one was really taking any notice of that; they were all putting their noses up in the air and sniffing like a dog trying to pick up a scent.

'Ooh, that's lovely,' the producer called out. 'Do you know what the perfume is called? I might get some.'

'I wouldn't do that if I were you,' Dad replied, walking to the front of the stage. 'Its industrial strength, people would smell you a mile away. I take it that the trial is a success then?'

'It certainly is for me,' replied the producer. 'What about everyone else?'

All the other members of the 'audience' agreed that the perfume smelled lovely, and that it totally covered up the normally horrendous odour of Florence's trumps.

'In that case,' announced the producer. 'I can officially confirm that Florence will be allowed to compcte in the semi-final of "Now You're A Star!", in two days' time.'

And everyone cheered as loudly as a theatre full of people.

Florence was back in the semi-final.

CHAPTER NINETEEN

Two days later, Florence and her family were back at the same theatre for the semi-final. Once again, Grandma, Grandad, Sam and Mrs Walker were in the audience, as were the three men who had set up the perfume spraying equipment, *and* just about all of the children from Florence's school, with their parents. Florence was in the same large room backstage with Mum and Dad, although the room wasn't as crowded as there were only ten acts in each semi-final show. (There were four semi-final shows altogether, and the best two acts from each would go through to the Grand Final.)

Florence felt less nervous this time, as she now knew she could perform on stage in front of a large audience, *and* she no longer had to worry about what people would think about her trumping, because everyone *loved* it. She was to be the seventh act on, so she sat and watched the first five acts on the big screen with Mum and Dad. Again, after every act Dad said, 'You're better than them,' and *that* started to make Florence feel nervous again. There was another ten-year-old girl who sang with a very powerful voice, a man who sang with an even more powerful voice, a magician, a ventriloquist, who the head judge Nigel didn't really like (possibly because the dummy looked like him) and a dog doing tricks, which Nigel loved.

When the dog act had finished, the same man as before, wearing the same crumpled t-shirt as before, came to take Florence to the side of the stage with Mum and Dad. While they were waiting, he told Florence he thought she was brilliant and not to worry about the smell because the perfume system was all set up and ready to go. Then there was a huge roar from the audience as the sixth act finished performing – it was a team of acrobats – and Florence waited quietly and nervously, while all of the judges told the acrobats how good they were and hoped they'd get through to the final. As soon as the acrobats had left the stage 'crumpled t-shirt man' said, 'Off you go then, good luck,' and after hugs from Mum and Dad, Florence walked out towards her two microphones in the centre of the stage, holding tightly on to her flute.

The audience rose to their feet and gave her a huge round of applause, even before she started! They were so intent on watching Florence, that hardly any of them noticed the high poles appearing at each side of the stage. Nigel waited for the applause to stop and then said, 'Hello, Florence. The audience seem to like you.' This brought another round of cheering from the audience. 'I hear there've been a few comments about your... "trumpeting", but they've all been sorted out, yes?'

'Yes,' replied Florence. 'My daddy did it.'

'Good for Daddy,' said Nigel. 'So what are you going to play for us today?'

'I'm going to play the "Flight of the Bumblebee".'

'I don't think I know that one,' Hughie chimed in. 'Is it one of Ed Sheeran's?'

The whole place erupted with laughter and Florence looked puzzled before answering, 'No, Rimsky-Korsakov.'

'Never mind Hughie, Florence,' said Nigel. 'Away you go then. And good luck.'

Florence took a deep breath, raised her flute to her lips and, as she did so, a very fine mist, so fine that it was almost invisible, began to flow from each side of the stage. The audience didn't notice it, as they were all bracing themselves for the horrendous smell that would accompany Florence's trumpeting –

142

the boys in the audience were even looking forward to it. As soon as she began to play the flute the audience clapped and cheered, although there were a few puzzled looks when they noticed a lovely perfume sort of smell. They soon forgot about this however, when Florence began her 'trumpeting' of the sound of the bumblebees, which was so realistic that many people started waving their arms around trying to swat the bees they thought were flying around them! Eventually, they realised that the bumblebees were simply Florence 'playing her bottom', and they roared their approval even more loudly.

Meanwhile, the judges, who had also been prepared for the horrendous odour, soon put down their handkerchiefs when they smelled the beautiful perfume instead. But then they picked them up again to try to wave away the non-existent bumblebees. When Florence completed her performance the audience burst into an enormous round of applause, which went on and on and on. Florence bowed once but then stood there with an embarrassed smile on her face. Eventually, Nigel raised his arms to get the audience to quieten down. Once they had, he said, 'Well, Florence, I was right – they do like you.' Another cheer from the audience. 'What did you think of that then, Hughie?'

'I think you're amazing, Florence. You really made that tune your own,' Hughie said. 'It was a great choice of music. And you smell amazing!'

'That wasn't me. That was the perfume coming out of the top of those poles,' said Florence, pointing at each side of the stage. They were my daddy's idea.'

'Well, they were a wonderful idea,' said Hughie. In the wings, Dad whispered, 'You hear that? A wonderful idea.'

'Well they were,' Mum whispered back.

'You are *so* talented,' said Nina taking over the commenting from Hughie. 'That is an extremely difficult piece to play and yet you played your two "instruments" effortlessly. I honestly don't know how you can play such a tune from your bottom *and* make it sound *exactly* like a bumblebee, never mind do it at the same time as playing the flute so perfectly. And your dress is absolutely lovely.'

'Thank you,' said Florence politely.

'Yes, you look *so* sweet,' said Amelia. 'The pale blue in your dress really brings out the blue in your eyes. And you play so beautifully. I really don't know what else to say. You have taken my breath away. But you must give me

144

the name of the perfume coming out of those nozzles. It's lovely.'

'You know what?' said Nigel, taking over from Amelia. 'You are why we do this show year after year. It's discovering amazingly talented people like you that keeps me coming back to do it. And you know what? Some people say that we should have a lower age limit on this show of sixteen, but you are proof that that would be wrong. We would never have discovered you. But we have, and the world is a better place because of it. And if the public don't vote you through to the final then I'll... never do this show again.'

'Don't tempt them,' Hughie chimed in from the other end of the judges' panel.

Nigel laughed and said, 'Shall we? Hughie?'

And Hughie said, 'Florence, Now-'

And Nina said, 'You're-'

Amelia said, 'A-'

'Huge ginormous, amazing Star!' said Nigel. 'Well done, Florence.'

Then Florence left the stage, smiling and waving at the cheering audience and jumped into Dad's arms, saying, 'Thank you, thank you Daddy. It worked!'

'Of course it worked,' replied Dad. 'I'm a genius. Even your mummy thinks so.' Then they went back to the big room where all of the other acts gave Florence a big round of applause and they all watched the three other acts that still had to perform. When they'd all finished, they were all given some food and drinks, and they chatted to each other while they waited for the results of the 'Public Vote'. Everyone was telling Florence that she was bound to get through to the final, but she wasn't sure if they meant it, because she said the same thing back to whoever she was talking to. The public only had an hour to vote, but it seemed more like a week to Florence and the other acts, who soon ran out of conversation, and sat waiting nervously to be called back to the stage.

Finally, 'crumpled t-shirt man' came in and asked everyone to follow him – the results were in! Each act was told precisely where to stand on the stage behind the enormous curtain shielding them from the audience. When the curtains opened there was huge roar from the audience, and the show's presenter, Daniel O'Bleary, had to wait for a few moments before he could begin to announce the results. He started with the act who had finished tenth and worked his way up. Each time he announced a name, the spotlight on that act would go out and the audience would go, 'Ah'. Florence stood there with her eyes closed, expecting her name to be called out every time. But of course, it wasn't. Now, Daniel was down to the last three. He would only announce one more name and if it wasn't 'Florence' then she would be through to the Grand Final. She screwed her eyes tightly shut as the presenter said, 'And the act who finished third tonight and is therefore *not* going through to the final is...F...'

The audience gasped. Mum and Dad looked at each other in horror.

'Finally going to be announced after the break!' said Daniel. There was a break for adverts! There always was; and every week the audience forgot, and let out a huge groan. So, Florence, Mum and Dad, and all of her friends, as well as the other two acts who had not yet been eliminated, had a very nervous five-minute wait until the show came back on the television. After what seemed like an age, Daniel O'Bleary welcomed everyone back to the show, and began his announcement again. 'The act finishing third tonight, and therefore *not* going on to the Grand Final next week, is...' he seemed to wait for ages before completing the announcement, but it was only a few seconds, until he said, 'John Watkinson! Sorry, John.'

The audience clapped and cheered as John was congratulated on getting that far, while Florence and the group of acrobats jumped up and down in celebration. Then the show's presenter talked to Florence and the acrobats, congratulating them and wishing them luck in the Grand Final.

Florence had done it! She was in the Grand Final of, 'Now You're A Star!'

CHAPTER TWENTY

Florence's semi-final had been the first one, and there were three more to go before the Grand Final, which would be in a big theatre in London the following weekend. It happened to be half-term, so Florence had almost a whole week to practice and make sure she ate plenty of sprouts. The next morning, after Florence had her 'training breakfast' of sprout porridge – a special dish invented by Dad - Mum went out shopping to stock up on the magical green vegetable, leaving Florence to practice in her room. Florence was still practicing when Mum returned, so she didn't hear Mum drop the shopping in the kitchen, pick up the phone and take it into the dining room, which just happened to be the room furthest away from Florence's bedroom.

She dialled a number, 'Dave?' she said when her call was answered. 'Something terrible's happened!'

'Oh, my god, what? Has there been an accident? Are you all right?' asked Dad.'

'No, everyone's fine. It's...' Mum paused to take a breath. 'It's the supermarket: they've run out of sprouts!'

'What? Is that *all*, Claire? Well, go somewhere else then,' he replied.

'I have, Dave,' said Mum. 'I've been all over town. There are no sprouts anywhere in the Stockport area. What are we going to do? I daren't tell Florence, she'll be distraught!'

'I don't know,' replied Dad. 'I'll have to think about it. Perhaps there's something else she can eat. What about cauliflower? That works for me.'

'She doesn't *like* cauliflower,' Mum replied.

'She didn't like *sprouts*,' Dad pointed out.

'Well, we may have to try it, if we can't get any sprouts,' said Mum. 'I'll see you later.'

'Yes,' said Dad. 'Meanwhile, I'll see if I can find some sprouts. I'll ring round our other branches. There must be some sprouts somewhere in the country. Perhaps I can get them couriered over to us.'

That evening, Florence sat down for her tea with the family, and looked down at her plate in bewilderment. 'Mummy,' she said.

'Where are my sprouts? And why have you given me cauliflower? You know I don't like it.'

'I'm sorry, darling,' replied Mum. 'I couldn't get any sprouts today. Everywhere has run out.'

'But what about my trumping?' said Florence, distraught (her mummy had been right about her reaction). 'I *need* sprouts to play the trumpet!'

'I've *told* you,' said Mum. 'There aren't any in the shops. Apparently everyone has been buying them to try to be able to play like you. You've started a craze.'

'Mummy's right,' agreed Dad. 'I've rung round all of our branches all over the country, and the whole place has run out of sprouts. They've never seen anything like it. You'll have to try cauliflower, and if that doesn't work, we'll have to try cabbage.'

'Cabbage! Yuk!' said Florence.

'Come on, sis,' said Sam, trying to cheer her up. 'Give the cauliflower a try. Remember Christmas, when you tried just a slither of a sprout, and fell in love with them. Do the same with the cauliflower.'

Florence looked at her brother. She *did* remember Christmas. She *had* hated sprouts.

Perhaps it *would* be the same with cauliflower. She nodded, and picked up her knife and fork, cut off a tiny piece of cauliflower, lifted her fork up to her mouth and slowly pushed it in. Everyone watched intently as she began to chew, and her expression changed from one of apprehension to one of pleasure. She *did* like cauliflower after all.

'Right,' said Dad. 'Everyone give their cauliflower to Florence; let's get that pressure building up so that she can blow her own trumpet.'

So they all scraped their cauliflower on to Florence's plate until there was a huge mound of the stuff, and she tucked in with a big smile on her face. She couldn't wait to practice after tea. She needed to know if cauliflower trumps would sound the same as sprout ones. Perhaps the tone would be different.

The whole family were just as keen to know the answer to that particular question, so they all gathered in the living room to listen to the cauliflower-induced trumpet. Florence set up her music stand by the window, although they left the window closed, thinking that cauliflower trumps couldn't be any worse than sprout ones, and she began to play. She decided to start with something simple – the carol she'd played last Christmas when she'd discovered her special talent, 'Ding Dong Merrily On High'. Her small audience waited expectantly for the trumpet to start.

But it didn't.

When Florence reached the trumpet part she tried to 'blow', and indeed did blow, but so little came out that it hardly made a sound. Dad's and Sam's trumps were louder!

'I can't do it!' Florence said, horrified. 'I don't have enough puff!'

'Oh no,' said Dad. 'Perhaps you need more cauliflower. Do we have anymore, Claire?'

'No,' replied Mum. 'I'll have to get some more tomorrow.'

'Tomorrow?' cried Florence. 'But I need to practice now!'

'I'm sorry, darling,' said Mum. 'But you'll have to wait. Don't worry, I'll buy all the cauliflower in the supermarket. I won't risk running out before the Final.'

'But what if it doesn't work, no matter how much cauliflower I eat?' said Florence.

'Oh, it'll work all right,' Dad reassured her. 'Won't it, Sam?'

Sam nodded. 'Of course it will,' he said. 'You just have to eat enough.'

So the next day, Mum came back from the supermarket with, quite literally, a whole car full of cauliflower, and she presented Florence with a plate of cauliflower cheese big enough to get in the 'Guinness Book of Records': it was so high that Florence could barely see over the top of it.

But even that wasn't enough, still her 'trumpet' was barely audible – a mouse's trump would be louder. It seemed that no amount of cauliflower would be enough to produce Florence's trumpet playing. Only sprouts would do.

And there were no sprouts left in the whole country.

CHAPTER TWENTY-ONE

Florence went to bed feeling extremely glum, and it took her a long time to get to sleep. She was going to look very silly in the Grand Final, if all she could do was play her flute. Meanwhile, downstairs, Mum and Dad put the television on to watch the 'News', and sure enough there it was – the main headline: the United Kingdom had run out of sprouts. Or at least all the shops had. It turned out that someone had been buying up all of the sprouts in the famers' fields, so that none of the shops could restock.

'Someone's trying to stop Florence getting any sprouts!' Dad gasped. 'Someone's sabotaging her!'

'You mean they don't want her to win, "Now You're A Star!"?' said Mum.

'Exactly!' said Dad.

'But who? Why?' said Mum.

'Don't know,' Dad replied. 'Perhaps... oh, hang on, look at this.'

A reporter, wearing a black ski-jacket, had appeared on the TV screen, standing in a field of sprouts, holding a microphone. 'I'm standing in a field full of sprouts,' he said. 'And yet, in all of our shops, all across the country, the shelves are empty. I have with me, David Baird, the farmer who owns this land and these sprouts. Tell me Mr Baird, why are our shelves empty of sprouts, when you have literally millions of them in your field *ready* to be picked, sold, and eaten?'

The reporter then thrust his microphone quite aggressively at the farmer, who stepped back in surprise, but managed to compose himself and reply, 'Well, you say they're my sprouts but... they're not anymore. They've all been bought, and I can't sell'em to anyone else.'

'You mean someone has bought *all* of your sprouts and you have none left to sell to the supermarkets?' asked the TV interviewer.

'That's right,' replied the farmer. 'I thought it were a bit strange; what with the price of sprouts rocketing after that little girl were on that show playing her bottom... after *eating* sprouts. Everybody wants 'em now, but my buyer won't sell 'em. Can't understand it. He could make a fortune.'

'And who is your buyer, Mr Baird?' asked the reporter.

'I'm afraid I can't tell you that,' replied the farmer. 'It's in my contract. He wishes to remain anonymous.'

'And there you have it, Huw,' said the reporter, looking back at the camera. 'It's the same all over the country. All of the sprouts, on all of our farms, have been bought up by an anonymous buyer, who is refusing to sell them to the supermarkets. Martin Simpson, BBC News, in a field of sprouts.'

The TV picture once again showed the studio news reader, who said, 'We can now go to our investigative reporter Matthew Jackman, who has been trying to discover the identity, and indeed the motive, of this mystery sprout – buyer. What have you got for us, Matthew?'

'So, Huw,' said the reporter. 'I'm standing outside this office-block in the centre of London, having just spoken to the man we believe to be at the centre, and in fact the cause, of this controversy. The gentleman in question is Mr Simon Waller. He's a multi-millionaire, believed to be worth in excess of five-hundred-million pounds, and our investigations have revealed that he has been very active in the sprout market over the last couple of days.'

'Interesting, Matthew,' said the studio newsreader. 'But what possible motive could Mr Waller have for buying up all the sprouts in the country, and then not selling them to the supermarkets for vast profits?'

'So, Huw,' replied the reporter standing in the cold and dark outside an office in the middle of London. 'It turns out that Mr Waller is the father of little Sophie Waller, the nine-year-old singer who, last night, reached the Grand Final of "Now You're A Star!". And of course, the current favourite to win that final is Florence Foulger, the flatulist and flautist, who, apparently, needs to eat mountains of sprouts to provide the wind to blow her "trumpet".'

'So you suspect Mr Waller of foul play, do you Matthew?' said Huw.

'So, Huw, it's not for me to comment on the morals of the case,' replied Matthew Jackman. 'But here's what Mr Waller had to say when we caught up with him on his way into his office, earlier today.'

The TV now showed Matthew Jackman standing outside the office in daylight, holding his microphone. A tall man in a smart, shiny, grey suit, with an open-necked shirt, his dark hair slicked back, carrying a black briefcase was approaching the office-block. As soon as he noticed the reporter he began to walk more quickly with his head down. The reporter moved towards the approaching man and, thrusting his microphone forward, he said, 'So, Mr Waller, is it true that you have bought up every single sprout in the country?'

'No comment,' came the reply.

'So, Mr Waller, is it true that you will not allow your suppliers to sell the sprouts to the supermarkets?' asked the reporter.

'No comment,' came the reply.

The reporter tried again. 'So, Mr Waller, is it true that you have done this to give your daughter, Sophie, a chance to beat Florence Foulger in the Grand Final of, "Now You're A Star!"?'

'No comment,' came the reply.

Finally, the reporter said, 'So, Mr Waller, don't you agree that this would be a very unfair and nasty thing to do? To use your vast wealth to sabotage the chances of a highly talented ten-year-old little girl?'

Mr Waller stopped in his tracks and, glowering at the reporter, snarled, 'And don't *you* think it's unfair that my little Sophie should have to compete against someone who is taking performance-enhancing chemicals to help her win?'

'*Performance-enhancing chemicals*?' said the reporter. 'They're *vegetables*!'

'Everything's a chemical,' replied Mr Waller. 'And if they are taken to enhance performance they should be banned.'

'So you admit you have bought up all the sprouts to stop Florence Foulger competing?'

'NO COMMENT!' screamed Mr Waller, before disappearing through the office-block doors.

The reporter turned to the camera and said, 'So, Huw, make of that what you will. Matthew Jackman, BBC News, in the cold and dark, in London.'

'So that's what's happened,' said Dad. 'We really have been sabotaged.'

'What are we going to do?' asked Mum. 'We can't let him get away with it.'

'Keep trying cauliflower, I suppose; lots of it,' said Dad. 'And if that doesn't work, cabbage.'

So the next day, Florence had cauliflower for breakfast and lunch, and when that didn't work, she ate cauliflower *and* cabbage for tea: all to no avail.

There were only three days to go to the Grand Final, and Florence couldn't trumpet a note!

CHAPTER TWENTY-TWO

Once again, Florence had gone to bed in tears. She'd been eating cauliflower all day and had even tried that horrible cabbage, but she still couldn't play her 'trumpet'. Once again, Mum and Dad sat in the living room watching the News, wondering what to do next. There was something on about the European Parliament in Brussels, but neither of them was taking much notice, until Dad suddenly said, 'That's it! I'm going upstairs to pack a bag.'

'Why?' asked Mum. 'Where are you going?'

'Brussels,' replied Dad.

'To the European Parliament?' queried Mum. '*They* won't do anything.'

'No, not the European Parliament,' Dad replied. 'Florence needs Brussel sprouts and they're bound to have some in Brussels. I'll get a van from work tomorrow; get the ferry over; buy a van load of sprouts; be back on Saturday - in plenty of time for Florence to have sprouts for tea. Then she can have them on Sunday as well, before the final, and she'll be fine.'

'You do know they speak French in Brussels?' Mum pointed out. 'And you don't.'

'Of course I do,' replied Dad. 'Bonjour, où est la gare? Je voudrais deux timbres, première classe, s'il vous plaît.'

'Dave,' sighed Mum. 'You're driving there, so why on Earth would you need to know where the railway station is, *or* want two first class stamps?'

'You never know,' replied Dad. 'Don't worry, I'll be fine.'

'Are you sure?' said Mum.

'Do you have a better idea?' Dad asked.

Mum shook her head, so they both went upstairs and Dad watched while Mum packed his bag, because, as Mum said, he couldn't be relied on to remember everything.

The next evening, while she was eating another combination of cauliflower, cabbage and broccoli, in the hope it would produce some trumpet sounds, Florence asked, 'Where's Daddy?'

'He's had to go to Belgium,' Mum replied, not wanting to get Florence's hopes up unnecessarily.

'Belgium? What for?' asked Florence.

'Work,' replied Mum. 'Don't worry, he'll be back tomorrow, in plenty of time to come to London with us on Sunday.'

'There won't be any point in going if I don't get some sprouts,' said Florence, sadly.

'Nonsense,' said Mum. 'You can always just play the flute. You'll still be brilliant.'

'Mum's right, Florence,' said Sam 'You're bound to get the sympathy vote, now everyone know what that Waller bloke has done.'

'I don't *want* the sympathy vote,' replied Florence. 'I want the "best performer" vote.' And once again Florence went to bed feeling very, very sorry for herself.

Shortly after Florence had gone to bed, Mum rang Dad to ask if he'd managed to find any sprouts.

'No, I've had a nightmare of a day,' he said. 'Seems everyone over here has been watching Florence on tele, and they've had a genuine run on sprouts. You can't get them for love nor money.'

'What are you going to do?' Mum asked anxiously.

'I've got the address of a little farm about a hundred kilometres outside Brussels. Apparently, he doesn't supply the supermarkets, so I'm hoping I can get some from him. Whatever happens, I'm getting the ferry back tomorrow afternoon. I'll be back home late evening.'

The next morning Mum told Florence Dad had been delayed, but was due back that evening, in time to go to London on Sunday with them.

'Doesn't matter anyway,' mumbled Florence. 'There's no point.'

Mum gave her daughter a sympathetic smile but said nothing, and then spent the day waiting anxiously for a phone call from Dad to confirm that he'd bought some sprouts and was on the ferry.

The phone call finally came in the early evening.

'Dave!' said Mum. '*Please* tell me you've got some sprouts.'

Dad sighed wearily, 'I've got a van full,' he said. 'But I've also got a puncture, and I've

165

missed the ferry. I'll have to get the overnight one and meet you in London at the hotel.'

'Oh, you poor thing,' said Mum. 'You sound exhausted.'

'I am,' replied Dad. 'But at least I've got the sprouts. You contact the hotel, and tell them we'll want them to cook the sprouts for Florence tomorrow afternoon. I'll get there as soon as I can.'

Mum decided not to tell Florence immediately, as she knew it would make her too excited to sleep, so she waited until the following morning.

'That's brilliant!' said Florence, when Mum told her the news. 'My daddy's so clever.'

'He certainly is,' replied Mum. 'Come on, let's get to the station and get on that train.'

Which is exactly what they did. So a few hours later Florence, Mum, Grandma, Grandad, Sam, and Mrs Walker, were walking into the special hotel the television company had booked for all of the contestants to stay in. And while they waited for Dad to arrive, Mum had a word with the hotel chef, who said he would be delighted to cook up whatever sprout-based dish Florence might want.

Meanwhile, Dad had disembarked from the ferry and was speeding along the motorway with a satisfied smile on his face and a van-full of 'trumpet fuel'. And I do mean speeding.

So it's not surprising that he soon heard a police siren and saw blue flashing lights in his rear view mirror. He knew immediately that he was in trouble and muttered things under his breath that young children shouldn't hear, as he pulled over on to the hard shoulder.

When the police car had stopped in front of him, Dad wound his window down, as he watched the grumpy looking traffic officer walking towards him.

There was no way he would get the sprouts to the hotel in time now. And there was no way that Florence would win 'Now You're A Star!'.

CHAPTER TWENTY-THREE

'In a hurry are we, sir?' asked the traffic policeman sarcastically, raising an eyebrow in Dad's direction.

'Well yes, I am, as a matter of fact,' replied Dad. 'You see...'

The policeman held up his hand to stop Dad in mid-sentence, 'I'm afraid whatever you're going to say can be no excuse for speeding, sir. Don't tell me. Let me guess: wife having a baby, is she?'

'No!' cried Dad, frustrated by the time being wasted. 'My daughter is competing in the final of "Now You're A Star!" tonight! And she needs the sprouts I have in the back of this van so that she play her bottom!'

The policeman's mouth dropped open. 'Your little girl is "Florence the Flatulistic Flautist"? *My* little girl thinks she's great,' said the policeman. 'She even eats her vegetables now, because of Florence!'

'That's very nice to know,' replied Dad, not sounding very interested in the policeman's daughter's diet. 'But I still need to get these sprouts to my daughter.'

'Don't you worry about that, sir,' said the police officer. '*I'll* get you there on time. Follow me.' He turned to dash towards his car, before stopping, turning back to Dad, and asking him where he was going.

Dad replied with the name of the hotel, and the policeman said, 'Right, follow me!' this time running all the way back to his car, jumping in, starting up his siren, and then driving past Dad waving for him to follow. Dad loved it, as he shot along in the outside lane, pretending that he was Lewis Hamilton in a Grand Prix.

By the time he and his police escort entered the London suburbs, Dad was back on schedule. The police car sirens were off now most of the time, only blaring out when needed to disperse the traffic in front of them. Eventually however, even the sirens couldn't clear the way, as they hit a solid wall of cars in front of them. Normally, Dad would have blown the van's horn in a completely pointless gesture of frustration, but as the car in front of him contained the helpful police officer, he decided to refrain. The policeman appeared at the side of Dad's van – not by magic, he had walked – and Dad wound his window down.

'Sorry, sir,' said the officer. 'There's no way I can make a path through this lot. There's been an accident in the middle of some roadworks just round the corner, and there's no way round it.'

'Great!' said Dad, obviously not meaning it. 'What am I going to do? Florence needs this sprouts!' He looked down at his watch and sighed. 'There's only one thing for it,' he said. 'I'm going to have to run the rest of the way.'

'Really?' replied a surprised policeman, who was unable to stop himself staring down at Dad's tummy, which was clearly straining to escape from the confines of his shirt.

'Nothing else I *can* do,' said Dad, throwing open the van door causing the policeman to jump back.

'OK,' said the police officer, as he watched Dad open the back door of the van and lift out a crate of sprouts. 'Leave me the van's keys and I'll sort it out for you. Ring this number and you can pick them up later,' added the officer, handing Dad a business card.'

'What? Oh, er, thanks,' Dad replied. He wanted to shake the policeman's hand, but he was already holding a crateful of sprouts – Dad not the policeman – so he simply said, 'Right,

I'd better get going,' and looked up and down the street before staring at the policeman with a helpless look on his face.

The officer understood instantly. 'That way,' he said, pointing. 'To the next corner, turn left and keep going: you can't miss it.'

So Dad set off at a jog, wearing a long-sleeved pale blue shirt and the dark blue trousers and nicely polished shoes that he usually wore when he was going to a posh restaurant with his wife: not the sort of clothes to wear for running. But *that* didn't slow him down as he dodged between the crowds of people who seemed to be sauntering along, *intentionally* getting in his way. No, what slowed him down was his lack of fitness (as deduced by the policeman) and he had barely reached the corner at which he was to turn left, when he had to stop and put the sprouts down on the pavement, so that he could rest his hands on his knees and draw in huge lungfuls of air.

But putting a crateful of sprouts down in the middle of a very busy pavement turned out not to be Dad's brightest ever idea. And, in under ten seconds, a young man, who had been paying too much attention to his mobile phone, while he texted his girlfriend to say that he'd just seen some random bloke running past him with a crateful of sprouts, tripped over the said tray and sent himself, and the sprouts, all over the pavement.

If he hadn't still been gasping for breath, Dad would have shouted a lot more than he did at the unfortunate young man, but instead, he crawled and groped around between the other pedestrians' legs, picking up and returning the sprouts to the crate, while the young man picked *himself* up and, without a word of apology, strode off, whilst texting his girlfriend that she'd *never* guess what had just happened.

Dad grabbed the now half-full crate of sprouts and set off at a jog once more, weaving in and out of the crowds of pedestrians as carefully as he could. *Why did nobody ever look where they were going?*

Eventually (it seemed like an age, but was actually only about five minutes) Dad arrived at the hotel and stumbled up the two or three steps to the door, unable to draw in enough breath to speak, and sat down. Fortunately, the police officer had had the foresight to ring the hotel and warn them of the impending arrival of a load of sprouts. So Dad was met at the door by Mum, who took the sprouts off him and passed them to a waiter to take to the chef for cooking.

Dad had done it! He'd saved the day. Soon, Florence would be tucking into a huge portion of delicious green spherical vegetables and would be ready for the Grand Final.

And, before Dad had recovered enough to stand up, he saw the very same policeman who had given him the high-speed escort, driving past, waving and giving him the 'thumbs up'. The accident had been cleared and the traffic was moving again: Dad needn't have done all that running after all!

CHAPTER TWENTY-FOUR

Florence woofed the sprouts down – three platefuls - in record time, and had just enough time to get ready for the Grand Final.

All of the acts were introduced together to the audience at the beginning of the show (Florence, of course, received the biggest applause) and then had to wait in a large room backstage while each act performed. As always happens in these sorts of things, all of the contestants were brilliant and the judges told them so. Florence was on last, and was feeling very nervous. Every act performed better than ever; surely one of *them* would win. What if the sprouts didn't have enough time to work? She soon found that she didn't need to worry about that, as small trumps began to sneak out – silently. The other acts and their close families began to move further away from Florence, as the smell permeated through the room. And no matter how hard she tried, Florence couldn't stop the popping of her bottom. It must have been because she was so nervous. Now she had something else to worry about – what if she ran out of wind before she started 'trumpeting'?

She became desperate for the all the others acts to finish, and she found herself willing the judges to stop going on about how good everyone was, so that she could get out on stage before she ran out of 'puff'.

When it was her turn, Florence almost ran to the centre of the stage and when Nigel Barlow welcomed her and asked her how she was, she replied, speaking extremely quickly, 'I'm very well, thank you Mr Barlow, but can I just start? You see I've not been able to get any sprouts for days - until this afternoon, when my Dad got a police escort when he was bringing them back from Brussels, after he was stopped for speeding on the motorway and...'

She'd been hopping from one foot to the other as she clenched her bottom trying to control her trumps, but one sneaked out and the sound was picked up by her 'trumpet' microphone. Florence was horrified but Hughie just said, 'Sounds like you're tuning up there, Florence.'

Florence blushed and started to reply, 'No, I -' but she was interrupted by Nigel, who held up his hand and said calmly, 'Florence, why don't you just play for us?'

So Florence did, and as soon as she let out her first trumpet note, which sounded as sweet as the proverbial nut, she knew that she had enough 'puff', and everything was going to be all right. The crowd clapped and cheered as she played 'The William Tell Overture' again, and when she finished she received the biggest ovation of the night. The applause seemed to go on forever.

Once again, Dad's perfume spraying equipment had done the trick and there were no obnoxious smells.

Yet again, Hughie said Florence was brilliant and had really made that tune her own, although Rossini may have had something to say about that if he were still alive.

Nina and Amelia were both in tears, and told Florence what a superb musician she was, and how beautiful she looked.

Nigel Barlow, the head judge, said, 'D'you know what I like about you, Florence? You're a brilliant little girl, who's had all sorts of problems to overcome to get to this final. There was the *stupid* 'Health and Safety' concerns, and then the smell complaints, and then the country ran out of sprouts! But you overcame all of that to give us a world class performance tonight. And you did it with the help of your family, and *that's* what this show is all about –

family. This show is for all the family, and I hope your family gets what it deserves – and that's a win tonight.'

The audience roared their approval of Nigel's comments, but he hadn't finished. When the noise subsided he continued, 'And d'you what else you've accomplished, Florence?' (He didn't wait for an answer.) 'You've made trumping respectable. Everybody's doing it now. Nobody's embarrassed. The whole country is making noises and smells, and apart from a quick, "excuse me" or a "well done" from someone nearby, we barely notice it anymore. So thank you for that, Florence. The world is a more relaxed place, thanks to you.'

The audience roared their approval again, although many of them tried to trump their approval instead, and a few of them had embarrassing *accidents*!

Needless to say, Florence won the Grand Final, receiving more votes than anyone else in the history of the competition. Little Sophie Waller apologised for her dad's behaviour, and said she was glad it hadn't ruined Florence's chances.

The first prize was a lot of money (£250,000) and a recording contract with Nigel

Barlow's record company. Of course, Florence's first album went triple platinum in a week, which means it sold an awful lot of copies. The vinyl version was extremely popular as that included a 'scratch and sniff' cover, as well as lots of sprout recipes. She was also asked to advertise a certain spherical green vegetable on television, and the adverts were so successful that the shops kept running out, even without some nasty man buying them all up.

As Florence grew up, she carried on playing her flute and trumpet, and making best-selling albums. She also took up athletics and, with the aid of her 'jet-propulsion' - enabled by her controlled, but powerful trumping - she became a world-record breaking sprinter, long jumper, high jumper and triple jumper. It took some practice, as she had to learn to release her 'power' steadily over quite long periods.

Florence wasn't allowed to compete indoors for obvious reasons.

So the next time your mum or dad tell you to 'eat your greens', make sure you do, you never know where it might lead.

THE END

PS: In case you're wondering, no, Victoria Beckham never produced a perfume called 'Parfum du Florence'.

Printed in Great Britain
by Amazon